Neal

Golden Streak Series

Book 3

KATHI S. BARTON

This is a work of fiction. Names, characters, places, and incidents are products of the author's imagination or are used fictitiously and are not to be construed as real. Any resemblance to actual events, locations, organizations, or person, living or dead, is entirely coincidental.

WCP

World Castle Publishing, LLC

Pensacola, Florida

Copyright © Kathi S. Barton 2013

Paperback ISBN: 9781629890265

eBook ISBN: 9781629890272

First Edition World Castle Publishing, LLC November 5, 2013

http://www.worldcastlepublishing.com

Licensing Notes

Cover: Karen Fuller

Editor: Eric Johnston

Chapter 1

Rayne put the tiny little plant in the dirt and pushed the soil around it. She had to get this and the seven more pots finished before she could leave, and it was already seven o'clock. One of these days, she was going to be able to afford some real help, but until then, she had to do the work herself. She heard her mom coming toward her and smiled when she smelled the food she'd brought with her.

"I knew I'd find you here. You should have left here over an hour ago. So as soon as five-thirty came and went, I gathered up your dinner…and here I am." Her mom sat on the stack of bags of soil and sighed. "If you'd let me help you, this would be much easier on you."

"It would, but you already work hard enough." She looked up at her mom as she took the sandwich from her. "How is it you can look so fresh after eight hours inside of a tight building when I've been outside most of the day and look like I've been run over? Twice."

"Because you have been outside all day working. I love that look on you. And not to mention you're not sleeping well. What's bothering you? Is it this new job you have?" She shook her head, then nodded. "Which is it, Rayne? The job or not."

"Not really the job. I can do that no problem. It's that Sindy. You remember her?" Her mom nodded. "Sindy recommended me for this, and I don't want to disappoint her. She said these people are nice, and she trusts them."

"And you don't trust them because...." Rayne looked at her. "Rayne, not all people are like the ones from where you worked. Most of them are very nice once you get to know them. You just haven't. Let people get to know you that is. I thought that once you got out into the public and away from that place, you'd start to realize that. I'm not wrong about this. You have to learn to trust people again."

She nodded. "I know you're worried about me, but I'm going to be all right." She broke the little plant at the base, and she stared at it. She heard her mother speak but not what she'd said until she looked up at her.

"Fix it." She shook her head. "You want to, darling. I can feel it. Fix the poor plant and put it in the dirt so it can grow. You didn't break it, just injured it a little."

She put it aside and reached for another plant. She wouldn't do it. Not again. Fixing things was what got her into trouble the last time, and she knew that she would have nowhere else to go if she was caught again. When her mom said she was going to look over the books for her, she nodded. Rayne planted the next pot before she picked up the dinner her mom had brought her.

There was a roast beef sandwich, chips, and three bottles of water. She'd also packed her an apple, an orange, as well as a banana. She probably knew that she'd skipped lunch too. Moaning as she bit into the heavy sandwich, she felt her belly rumble for more. She was halfway finished with the sandwich when she looked around. Picking up the little injured plant, she closed her eyes and let her power drift over it.

Setting it back in the little container, she finished her dinner and was picking up her second bottle of water when her mom came out of the office. She glanced at the flower but said nothing about it. Rayne was glad; she didn't want to have to explain that the little thing was calling to her. Calling to her as most of the greenery that she worked with did.

"You're about ten dollars short on your checking account again. I covered it." She started to protest, but her mom held up her hand. "I covered it. Now hush. I've also called the Hogans as well as the Sanders. Stupid jerks. They still haven't paid you, and they are now well past due. I put the fear of me in them, and the Hogans said they'd mail you a check tomorrow. I'm not holding my breath. Monday, I'm going by there and kicking their ass and taking back the planters they have. That Sanders person said some very unprofessional things, and I hung up. I think you need to hire yourself a lawyer."

Rayne snorted, and her mother laughed. "I can't afford to have a checking account. How on earth would I hire a lawyer? Besides, they'll just take more of the money I don't have and I'll still have people who owe me. And you will not go by there and get the stuff. I'll go. He might sic some dogs on me, and you know how much I hate dogs." Her mom laughed as she'd intended for her to.

Rayne was on the fifth pot when her mom left her. She said she had to go in early tomorrow and wanted to get to bed early. Rayne kissed her on the cheek and told her she loved her before she sat back down and continued with what she was doing.

It took her another three hours to finish the planters and clean up the mess. She was spraying the last of the dirt from the floor with the hose when she decided that she was going to make this new job work if it was the last thing she did. Besides, there was the money thing that she liked, too. Having it to pay bills and eat was something she felt strongly about. Locking up, she went to her little apartment in the back of the shop to rest up.

As soon as she entered her kitchen, she saw the notes that she'd taken when she'd talked to Sindy. They were of what the building that she said the Golden Towers wanted her to fix looked like. She'd never been in the building before, but it sounded cold and sterile. She sat down and started to sketch out some of the ideas she had.

There were five offices and the main lobby she might get to do. Sindy had told her that she would be in competition with three other florists to have the contract, and she was hoping that Rayne would get the job. So was she, but she wasn't holding out much hope. Two of the other florists were high-end like the building sounded to be, and the other one was "big box"—meaning they had really deep pockets. She did, too, she thought with a laugh, but there wasn't anything in them.

She was into the third drawing when her phone rang. Wondering who was calling her this late, she nearly didn't answer it until she saw who it was. She smiled as she answered the phone.

"Hi, Sindy, I was just thinking about you. Do you know if the building has direct or indirect lighting in the front of the building?" There was a long pause, and she wondered if she had mistaken who called her. Then Sindy spoke.

"I have no clue. Do you have any idea what time it is?" She said she didn't. "Then I'm glad I called you. You have two hours to get to the Golden building, or you're going to be disqualified before you get to wow them. Don't you ever look at a clock?"

"No, I don't." But she did start gathering up her notes to take with her, wondering why she was even bothering. "And thank you for the call. I should have gone to bed instead of playing with these drawings."

"You've been up all night again? Damn it, Rayne, what am I going to do with you? Your mother will be pissed when she finds out you've skipped sleeping again." Rayne had a feeling her mom already knew. "Get dressed and call me the moment you get there. I want to know what you're wearing, too."

Rayne supposed her jeans and tee-shirt that she'd worked in all night weren't going to cut it and told her she'd let her know. After hanging up, she went to her closet and looked at the collection of brightly colored tee-shirts she had and the five or six...no, just five pairs of jeans she had hanging next to them. Her last pair of pants was now in the laundry, as she had taken them off when she'd run through the apartment half-naked.

Closing her eyes, she pulled the first shirt off the hanger and went to the shower. She was in and out within ten minutes. She never understood why some people would take an hour to get ready to go somewhere when she could do it in fifteen minutes, even if she had to shave her legs. Laughing, she wondered what company would care if her legs were smooth or not, picked up her files and her backpack with her laptop in it, and went to wait for the bus.

She was ten minutes early. This was good, she supposed, since the guard at the front desk had to make her a visitor's badge. He wanted more information than she'd had to give the bank when she'd applied for her loan. Not to mention he checked her bag like she was taking out trade secrets or something. Not that she had a clue what happened in this place, but she let him do it, even joking about the candy bar he'd discovered on the bottom.

"My lunch. Sometimes I forget to eat, and my mom is forever putting things in my pockets or, in this case, backpack in the event I get hungry." He grinned at her, then told her to have a seat. She went to the seats he indicated and watched the two women who were obviously her competition.

"This color on the walls is difficult to work with," the older woman said to the woman next to her scribbling notes. "They'll have to come up with a better color than brown to let me work in this stifled area. And make sure you tell them that the desk is in the wrong place."

Rayne looked at the desk and wondered what the hell that had to do with putting plants and flowers in here. She looked at the "stifling" walls and thought the tan was very nice and looked very good against the slate-covered flooring. She watched for a few more minutes as someone came out of the doors next to her. She watched as a beautiful woman, and a man led them out and to the desk.

More competition, she supposed. Rayne leaned back on the couch, which she discovered was more comfortable than her bed at home, and closed her eyes. She slipped away in seconds.

~~~

Brock looked at the girl and smiled. She was really out. He looked up at Stan, and he nodded. This was her. Brock reached down and touched her arm to wake her and to tell her that she needed to get going, that she'd missed her appointment, when he found himself on his back and a hand wrapped around his throat. He had a feeling if he moved to push her off him, she'd hurt not just him but her as well. He waited for her to realize where she was.

"I fell asleep." He nodded and lifted his hands up to show her he wasn't going to hurt her. "Did I hurt you?"

"No. I'm fine. I'm sorry that I startled you." She nodded and slipped off him, and when she stood up, offered him her hand. He took it even though he knew that he was much heavier than he looked, and more than likely, she wouldn't be able to lift him. But when he was suddenly standing, he looked down at her. Damn, she was strong.

"I had this appointment with…I can't remember now what his name was. I guess I fuc…screwed that up by taking a nap on the company furniture." She went back to the couch she'd been resting on and started gathering up her things. "I missed my bedtime last night because I'm a dork."

Brock liked her for some reason and didn't want her to leave without Bronwyn or Ryland at least getting to see her. She put her backpack on her shoulder and looked at him. He had to shake the feeling that she was as cute as she was pretty. *Weird combination,* he thought and laughed to himself.

"I can get my brother if you'll wait here." She looked at the desk where Stan and a couple of other guards were standing. They looked ready to do her harm but were waiting on him to give the signal. "Will you? Wait, I mean? They're not going to toss you out, I promise."

She turned back to him and smiled. Christ, he'd been wrong on both accounts. She was beautiful. "Nah. I should let these men stand down or whatever they're doing. I got some planters to steal back anyway for nonpayment."

She was walking to the desk when Bronwyn came out of the elevator. Brock waved her over just as the woman handed Stan her badge. She was nearly to the door when he caught up with her.

"This is my sister-in-law, Bronwyn Golden. She and my brother are the ones doing the hiring for the lobby. I take it that's what you're here for?" He smiled at her, and she frowned. "Are you?"

"Yes." She looked at him, then at Stan, before she hiked her backpack higher up on her shoulder. "I knew the rules, Mr.

Golden, and one of them was to be on time. I screwed up. I don't think it would be fair to the others for me to have special treatment because I fell asleep instead of doing what I should have been doing last night. I messed up. No harm, no foul."

She nodded at Bronwyn and started for the door. Bronwyn caught up with her this time and touched her arm. The woman jerked from her so quickly that Bronwyn took a step back and Stan and his two men forward. Something like a lightning strike arched between them.

"Christ." Bronwyn reached for her again when the girl backed up quickly. "I won't hurt you. I just… I can't believe what I felt. Did that come from you?"

The younger woman looked at him, then at the door, which was only about a foot away. She put her backpack in front of her like a shield and backed to the door. Brock didn't know what had happened, but he was willing to bet that Bronwyn did.

"Miss, I'd like to speak to you. I need to—" The woman shook her head at Bronwyn. "I swear to you that you'll not be treated any way but with kindness and—"

"I have to go. I'm sorry to have wasted your time, but I really need to get going. And nothing happened. It was…static electricity from the carpet." She moved to the revolving door just as Stan came to them. He handed Brock the badge she'd had on. She paled but kept moving.

"Your name is Rayne Morrow, and you work for The Pretty Flower?" She never stopped moving and didn't answer him. She was out the door before he could get an answer. He turned to look at the bare floors and then at Bronwyn.

"Why didn't she make her appointment?" Bronwyn watched the door go around and around quickly. "She was here, wasn't she?"

"She fell asleep on the sofa, she said. I guess she was up all night working and was tired. Stan told me about her when I came down to leave for lunch. I woke her, and she tossed me to the floor like I'd try to hurt her." Brock wondered if the door had ever gone that fast before and what she'd done to make it go around for so long. He knew why she'd done it—it was so they couldn't follow her—but not how she'd done it.

"I want to wait an hour and then go to her shop. Find out as much as you can about her, please, and let me know. I'll be in Ryland's office." She turned to the elevators but turned back. "Is she your mate, Brock, and did you touch her? Other than her touching you, did you touch her?"

"No to both questions. She had her hand around my neck, but I never…wait. She helped me up off the floor. I took her hand when she offered it." She shook her head. "I don't understand."

"She touched you, not the other way around." She smiled at him. "Don't touch her. And only take her hand if she touches you first, and only if you're sure she's okay with it. She might hurt you without meaning to."

It didn't take him long to find out enough to start him looking for Rayne. Stan knew her scent, or at least that of someone she knew. He told him about the other woman. A wolf.

"Older than this one but not by much, I'd say. Doesn't really look like her, so they can't be related. She's pack, the older woman. Her mate died some time ago, so she's not active in the pack, but she does attend the lunar meeting every time. Should be at one this weekend. Her name is Karin Hull. Nice lady."

Brock went to his office and had someone pick him up some lunch as he searched. He also had his and Neal's shared secretary, May Crawford, stop off at the county office to see what she could find out about the building Rayne was working from. His search on the shop made him smile. The person who had put this together had some skill and a great deal of humor. Some of the descriptions on what the shop could do were hysterical. His favorite one was about the recent remodel that had apparently been done.

"We've spent tones of dollars on the update and couldn't afford much more because buying this place drained us like a vampire would. Then we had to...you get the picture. Come on down and let us see how we can help you with your pot needs. (We mean the kind on your deck, not the kind you might be growing in your basement.)"

The owners' names were listed as simply R. Morrow and K. Hull. He did a search on Rayne and came up with all kinds of hits, but little to help him find out about the girl. He did find out she was a graduate, with honors, of the local university and that her education was centered on horticultural as well as animal husbandry. Odd combination, but he had a degree in criminal justice and Chinese, so he didn't think much of it. But the other woman, who was her mother, he supposed, was a different story. About her, there was a great deal.

Karin had hit the papers about twenty-six years ago when she'd been the daughter of a very wealthy family and had disappeared one night. The family had been very hushed about it until it came out a few months later that the girl, all of sixteen, had been disowned by the family for being pregnant. Her story, when she'd been asked later, was that she'd been kidnapped and raped repeatedly and that she'd not known her assailants.

Then there was a birth announcement, then a marriage about five years later to an Evan Hull. He had died about three years ago, and she'd been in the paper several times since as being a humanitarian and philanthropist. He pulled up pictures.

He could see where Stan would think that they weren't related.

Karin had light hair that looked to be very curly in all the pictures of her, while Rayne's was dark, a blue-black, and hung down her back in a straight line. Her mother's eyes were blue, but her daughter's were dark brown. Brock thought there could be a great deal of Native American Indian in Rayne, but her skin, like her mother's, was as creamy as milk. He looked at his watch, and as the last several sheets he'd had printed spit out of the printer, he wolfed down his sandwich and put the rest of the information in a folder. His secretary met him at the door as he was leaving.

"I found this at the county office for you as well as some information from a friend of mine at the collection bureau. You didn't find this from me, but the girl is having some major financial issues. Mostly nonpayments. But not due to her history but that of her clients. She is having some problems with five accounts. She's inquired as of the day before yesterday on how to get them turned in. The man had said all she needed to do was sign off on the contract, and they were ready. Nearly thirty grand is what these companies owe her."

"How did that happen?" He took the copies and looked them over. Then he looked up at her. "Sander's owes her almost twelve grand."

May nodded. "The other companies that she is trying to collect from are people we deal with too. Nate, my friend, said that one of them has owed her since she's opened, that he was her first client."

Brock went to Ryland's office to let them know what he'd found out, including what May had found out. Bronwyn was lying on the sofa in his brother's office, asleep, and he sat in the chair across from Ryland and handed him the file. He told him what else he'd found.

"I'd like to take a trip down there when you go. I want to get some things for the house, as well as see what she had to offer for her." They both looked at Bronwyn, who was struggling to sit up. At nine months pregnant, she wasn't moving as well as she had. Brock, for one, was worried about her exploding.

"I'm going?" She nodded. "Why? I don't think after what happened in the lobby, she's going to be all that thrilled to see either of us. And that door went around for twenty minutes after she left. Stan said when someone approached it from the outside, it stopped and has worked all right since. I'd hate to see what she'd do to us if we piss her off."

"Well, we'll just have to work really hard at not pissing her off," Bronwyn said, stood up, and smiled. "I'm going. If you don't want to go with me, I'll take Ally. She and I could have a great deal of fun there, I'm sure."

Brock nodded and reached for his cell phone. He called Stan and asked him to please bring his truck around. He put his phone away as Bronwyn was getting off hers. She was smiling. This was not going to be good.

"Ally is going as well. She's in the building with Alistair having lunch." She walked to Ryland and sat on his lap. "Tell me everything you know about her while we wait. And I heard you mention collections. Do you think we can help her by having Neal get on their asses?"

"I think we should see what we can find out as to why they aren't paying her. Could be she's done them a shitty job, and they refused on those grounds." Brock nodded at Ryland but didn't think he was right. He knew that Sanders could be a major prick when he wanted to be and wouldn't be surprised if he simply didn't pay her because he thought he could get away with it.

They left fifteen minutes later. The women were talking a mile a minute about what kind of flowers they were going to buy. Brock thought about how to ask Rayne out without touching her. But the more he thought about sleeping with her, the more creeped out he became. For some reason, he was beginning to think of her as a little sister and not a sex partner. He shuddered when he thought of her naked. Christ, he was going over the deep end here, and he'd just met her.

Chapter 2

Karin watched the store front as she looked over the bill that had come in the mail. She wished that her daughter would simply let her put some of her money in the business account, but she'd refused it. She told her that if she couldn't make this work on her own, then she might as well give it up. Other than her helping with the down payment and co-signing, she'd had little to nothing to do to help her.

But Rayne needed the income from the eight accounts that were past due before she could be in the black. And if it didn't happen soon, she might lose it all, starting with the place she lived. When the bell sounded, she looked up from the computer and smiled.

"Hello. Welcome." She handed the first woman a layout of the showroom and a flyer that Rayne had printed that morning. "We're having a sale on early bloomers. And trees today. If you need anything, just holler. I'll be right here."

The very pregnant woman nodded and moved to the violets near her. She was lifting one of the smaller pots up to smell it when the other woman stepped up beside her. It was then that Karin knew what they were. The man simply stood behind them.

"Is your daughter here?" The question from the man startled her somewhat, and when she stared at him, he repeated his question. She'd heard him but just wondered what he needed Rayne for.

"She's out doing some repossession of a couple of pots. Nonpayment." She had no idea why she said that and flushed. "She should be back soon. Do you know her?"

He nodded. "She came by this morning to see about doing the building for us. Golden Towers. Did she mention it? Or any of us?"

She had. But Rayne had only said that she'd not gotten the job because she'd fallen asleep on the couch and had missed her appointment. Rayne had said nothing about them coming here. Karin watched as the pregnant woman put five of the violets in her cart.

"Why are you here?" He raised a brow at her. She decided that she didn't care for him and looked at the three of them. "She works hard, and if you have a beef about something, then you can just leave here now. My daughter is a good...." She looked at the pregnant woman. "You touched her."

She looked like she'd come out on top, and Karin had a moment to worry when she nodded. "I had only meant to stop her from leaving so quickly. She had missed talking to us, and I wanted to see what she had to offer the building. The others hadn't worked out, you see. I'm Bronwyn Golden. This is my sister-in-law, Ally Golden, and my brother-in-law, Brock."

"Karin Hull. Rayne said that one of the women wanted the walls repainted and something done with the floors. Rayne said they were natural slate, and the color suited it." The woman nodded. "She didn't mention speaking to any of you and not that someone...that's why you're here. You think to profit off her and what you found out by touching her? Well, I won't have it. Nothing will happen to her again, do you understand me? I want you all to leave here right—"

"I don't want to hurt her or to profit from her. I just want to talk to her. See if...I don't know, talk to her." The company van pulled into the lot, and Karin tensed up. She had a feeling that Rayne wasn't going to be happy to see these people here any more than she was having them here.

Rayne got out of the van and started for the door when Karin saw her. Running to the door, she left the Goldens standing there as she went outside to help her. Someone had hurt her little girl.

"I'm fine. Stop fussing." There were times when Karin could kick herself for making her daughter so independent, and this was one of those times. "He wasn't too happy about me coming to get my merchandise. I guess I might have said something to piss him—"

Karin knew the moment that the others stepped outside with them. Her daughter's body went from trying not to lean too heavily on her to shoving her behind her, and her body became as stiff as a board. She also felt Rayne's power drift over her.

"We're only here to talk. I swear it." Bronwyn stepped forward slowly, and so did Brock. "My name is Bronwyn. From this morning, and I—"

"I know who you are. What do you want?" No one said anything as Brock stepped in front of Bronwyn. "If I had wanted to harm her, I would have done it already. I think you should leave now."

"Who hit you?" That same compulsion was there, but Karin could have told him he was wasting his breath. "Was it one of the people who owe you money? Sanders?"

Rayne's laughter was bitter and slightly manic. "So what if it was. And believe it or not, I don't need some big strong tiger and his ambush to take care of me." When Rayne reached for the nearest post, Karin realized how much dealing with these people was draining her in addition to however much she'd been hurt.

"You know what we are." Bronwyn smiled as she continued. "I remember now, you must be a friend of Sindy Wilson's. She's a friend of mine, too. She said you were going to come in today, but she never told me your name. She said that you'd told her that you didn't want an unfair advantage over the others. I'd like to see what you would have done for us."

"No." Karin wanted to smack her daughter but only stepped up beside her and wrapped her arm around her waist to help her inside. When she whimpered, she let her go immediately, and Rayne nearly fell over. The man leapt forward to catch her, and Karin stepped in front of him quickly.

"She'll kill you." He took a step back, and Karin turned to her daughter. "I can lift you, but you know I can't carry you far. Please, darling, I need to get you inside so I can see to you. May he help me?"

When Rayne nodded, Karin knew her daughter was in a great deal of pain if she was willing to allow a stranger to touch her. Karin turned to the man to caution him. He was looking at Bronwyn, and she knew that they were communicating. She said his name softly.

"You can lift her, but try to touch as little of her bare skin as you can. She's weak and might…you still might get hurt." He nodded and went to Rayne. When he lifted her, touching only her arms, she saw him stiffen. "I'm sorry. I would carry her, but I have a weak leg that prevents me from carrying her very far."

"I have her. And she's not hurting me. It's…she's very powerful, isn't she?" Karin nodded and led him back to the little two-room apartment at the back of the shop. Bronwyn said she'd watch the store until she returned.

The apartment was as neat as Rayne's shop and showroom were. There was nothing out of place in either room, and everything that couldn't be put away was in neat stacks for now. Her bed was made, as she knew it would be. She pulled the covers down so that he could put her down. He stood over her for several minutes before he turned to Karin.

"What is she?" he asked. Karin looked at her daughter, then up at him as he continued. "She tossed me off her today when I touched her arm. I thought it was because I startled her, but it was because I hadn't had her permission, wasn't it?"

"I need to check her wounds. If you wouldn't mind stepping out, I'll do that now." She reached down and pulled her blouse open. She nearly leapt on him for that, but his sharp intake of breath had her looking down, too. "Christ."

Someone had hurt her little girl and from the looks of it, had bruised a couple of ribs, too. Karin went to the bathroom to get a washcloth and came back in the room to see that Brock had removed her shoes and was tearing her pant legs up. There were bruises starting there as well.

"Do you know who did this?" Karin tried to ignore him, but she wanted someone to pay for what happened to her little girl. "Mrs. Hull?"

"She was going to see three people today. They owe her money, and she was going to see if she could collect at least some of it. And if that failed, she wanted to get her merchandise back. Nothing has worked so far with these people, and she's nearly broke." She wiped at the blood on her daughter's lip and saw that it was split open. "Someone hit her in the mouth. Why would they do that to her?"

By the time she'd finished cleaning Rayne up, the man had left, and Bronwyn and Ally had stepped in. The two women helped her take the rest of her ruined clothes off and redress her in an oversized tee-shirt like the ones that Rayne had been wearing to bed her entire life. They walked out of her apartment and to the shop, where Brock was manning the counter and helping a woman look over their map. She would have laughed at his expression of relief when he saw her if she hadn't been so pissed off. After the customer left, she was ready to close up and go back to Rayne.

"I think you people should leave. I appreciate your help with her, but I can take it from here." She started for the door. "And I would appreciate it if you'd keep whatever you think you know about us to yourself. Sort of you don't tell on me, and I'll keep who you are quiet as well."

"Is there a way you could show me what she was going to do for us?" Bronwyn picked up three more plants and added them to her overflowing cart. "I really didn't hire any of the others. The woman that had wanted me to change the color of the lobby said she had an idea in mind and that we'd have to work with her if we wanted her name attached to our building. I tossed her out on her ass immediately. The other two didn't even have a clue what they wanted to do, just that they thought that since they were a name brand, we should pick them for that reason alone."

"She had spoken to Sindy, and she'd had her take some pictures for her." Karin just wanted them gone and felt it didn't matter if they took the drawings or not. She dug them out of the trash and handed them to her as she rang up their purchases. "As soon as we're finished here, I would very much like for you to go, please. I need to get back to my daughter."

The total came to just under three grand. Not bad, she thought, for people who probably wouldn't have a clue what to do with their plants when they got them home. She took the credit card, hoping it went through, as Brock had already loaded everything in the back of his big truck. As Bronwyn signed the receipt, she looked at her.

"We won't hurt her or you," Bronwyn said. Karin nodded and took the signed slip. "I would like to speak to her again. Can you have her call me?"

"I can tell her you want to speak to her, but I wouldn't hold out any hope of her doing it. She's a little on the stubborn side." Bronwyn laughed. Karin followed her to the door. "Thank you for your help." As Karin closed and locked the door, she thought about the people who had just left and wondered how Rayne would feel about calling them back. Laughing, she knew that her daughter would have a fit.

~~~

Neal looked at the printouts that were handed to him, then up at his brother. He had to be kidding him. When Ryland sat down in the chair and waited, he looked harder at the paperwork.

"You don't think I have enough to do here that you go and dig shit out of the trash to bring me to work on?" Ryland nodded at him. "This one has mayonnaise on it. Seriously, who does this kind of crap to their records?"

"Bronwyn said she had dug it out of the trash and was pretty sure the woman hadn't realized she'd given it to her with the drawings she'd requested." Neal looked up from the dirty but otherwise neat row of numbers. "Can you tell me if those records say who is behind in their billing and how late they are?"

Neal nodded and wrote down the three names that he'd found right off. "There are actually eleven accounts that are past due as of now. These three...damn, this person must have had some accounting classes because this is perfect. Anyway, these three are over two hundred days past due. And the rest...the rest are coming up on ninety days. None of them, save one, has made a payment yet. Who do these belong to, and how do I get her to work for us?"

"Her name is Rayne Morrow, and as you probably surmised, she owns a plant place called The Pretty Flower. I don't know if she does her own books or her mom does, but I'm glad to hear that she's keeping good records." Neal barely heard him as he went down the neatly printed rows. He looked up at his brother when he was halfway down. "What did you find?"

"Another name, Sanders." His brother wasn't going to like this. He already hated Sanders with a passion. He told him. The two of them had been in a serious competition to hate each other since they'd encountered one another at a fundraiser and did their best to outbid one another on a piece of art that was Jules.

"I figured that. Brock had heard that he owed her some money." Ryland stood up to pace, and Neal laid the papers down. He wanted to get back to them. Hell, he wanted to meet the woman who had kept the records but waited on his brother.

"How do we get him to pay to an account that we don't have anything to do with?" Ryland said. Neal responded with the first thing that popped into his head, and Ryland laughed. "Okay, other than kidnapping him and taking it from his body a pound at a time. I was thinking more on the legal side for now."

"Would you consider becoming a partner with this shop owner? It looks like she's doing a steady business, and other than these accounts being seriously in arrears, she is making good money. Do you know how long she's been doing it?" Ryland told him about two years. "Then I'm even more impressed. She's making a major profit, and if she could get the cash from those three accounts, she'd be flying. Why the interest in a flower shop, Ryland? And don't tell me it's because she has something you want. You have everything."

"Bronwyn wants her to do the lobby for us," Ryland said.

"She has a good head on her shoulders for that too. You should see what she had in mind for us." Neal didn't really care what the lobby looked like but said nothing. "What would you do? I mean, how would you approach them in seeing if they needed a partner?"

He wouldn't take on a partner of any kind, not if she was doing as well as she was. But he could see where she'd need someone to help with the collections as well as billing. He wondered what they were doing about that when he realized that Ryland was saying something. He asked him to repeat it.

"I said, why don't you do it for me? She isn't too happy with Bronwyn or Brock right now, and maybe a fresh face would be just the thing." Neal was nodding before he could think it through. "Good. Oh, and Bronwyn said don't touch the younger woman useless she gives you permission. Something about her being a powerful being and will knock you on your ass like she did Brock."

Ryland was gone for a full five minutes before Neal thought about what he'd said. Someone had knocked Brock on his ass, and Ryland wanted him to go and see her? Not fucking likely. He was about to go after his brother when his phone rang. He picked it up with a bark of his name. His mom was not amused.

"You have a perfectly good first name. And saying 'Golden' like it's a command does not set well with me. If I had known that you all were going to use it like that, I wouldn't have agonized over first names at all and simply named you all Golden Golden." He smiled. "And the reason I called…. See what you've done? You've made me forget. And it is not my age creeping up on me either."

"I never thought it was," Neal said. "I was going to say, why don't you come and have breakfast with me? Then maybe in a more relaxed and calming place, you'll remember what is no doubt another brilliant idea, and I'll tell you what an awesome mom you are. Then, afterward, we can go out to The Pretty Flower and see if we can strike up a deal with the owner."

"Oh my, but aren't you the charmer. I think you're my favorite son today. Maybe even tomorrow as well if you pay for breakfast. And that's what it was. Not the breakfast part but the shop. I've heard Bronwyn speak of nothing else but the place. She also warned me that if I were to go and visit it I wasn't to touch the young woman. What do you suppose that means?"

He told her he'd been warned as well. "Let's go and see her first. Then maybe we can persuade her to eat with us. Two women on my arms as I go into a restaurant might make people forget that I'm a stodgy accountant and go out with me."

"You date a great deal, and we both know it. And as for the girl eating with us, I don't think that will work. From what I've heard, the girl is somewhat standoffish and is the only one working in her place except for her mother. Do you suppose that her mother despairs of her answering the phone in such a manner that it makes her cringe?"

"I'm sure she is a very sweet girl who loves her mother only about half as much as I love you." He heard her sigh and laughed. "I mean, who else invited you out to breakfast but your favorite son?"

"So you think. But I will take you up on the breakfast date. I want to try that new place on Indiana Street. It's called the Casual Diner. I love the name, don't you?" He told her he'd meet her in the lobby in twenty minutes. "Oh, and see if you can borrow that monster of Brock's. I may want to pick up a few things for the Memorial Day cookout at the house."

He called his brother, who said he didn't mind and was again told not to touch the girl. He was beginning to just want to touch her just to see what would happen. He was down in the lobby when his mom and Bronwyn showed up.

"I'm not going, so you can wipe that look off your face." Neal had to fight hard not to smile at his sister-in-law. "I'm headed to the doctor's, then on to a meeting with that idiot Sanders. He has to learn to behave himself, or I'm going to hurt him."

"I can go with you to the doctor's and the meeting. I don't want to have to have to bail you out of jail again. The last time it happened, I was told that they would take me into custody with you just to keep you in line." She turned to glare at her husband, Ryland, as he walked up behind her. "And then, if you're really good, I'll take you home and massage your poor feet."

Bronwyn was due in five days. None of them could believe that she'd made it this far, as she looked ready to blow up at any second. And her temper was just as bad. She wasn't taking well to the heat wave they'd been having, and if you were in a room she'd been in for more than an hour, you had to bring a coat. She was always burning up.

After a nice and hardy breakfast, he and his mother went to the shop. His brother was right about one thing, it was really nice. The displays on the outside of the building were bold and bright, and he wanted to load up one display and take it to his own house. It was so beautiful. And the strange part was, he didn't really care for flowers all that much.

They walked in to see someone at the counter and three more in line behind them. There didn't seem to be anyone at the cash register. He also noticed that while they did seem to be waiting, none of them seemed to be pissy about the wait. Then he saw the woman coming from a little alcove at the left.

"I'm sorry, David. She said that it would be at least another hour. Can you wait, or do you want her to bring it out to you? Rayne said she's really sorry, but she's been in that accident and all." She took his purchases and set them in a box.

"I'll wait. That way I can spend more money. Tell her I think she's really clever." When the woman started to protest, the man raised his hand. "I was kidding, Karin. I saw her, remember? And her mouth does not look like she was in an accident. I'd like to hit the person who would do something like that to her. I'll just keep looking around."

He walked away, and the woman rang up the other customers who were good-natured and seemed to know both Karin and Rayne, the mystery woman, very well. By the time she came from behind the counter again and approached them, his mom had a cart nearly full of baskets.

"Hello." He saw her hesitate, and when she did, he realized she was a wolf. No one had mentioned that to him, and he decided that the next time he saw Ryland, he was going to point out again how much he hated not having all the information up front. He also noticed that she was a good deal cooler than she'd been with the other customers.

"I'm Neal Golden, and this is my mom Sandra. We've stopped by to see you and Rayne. I believe that's your daughter's name." Karin shook her head before he even finished. "Please don't say no. I have a few things I'd like to discuss with her, one of which is her accounting. It's perfect."

He saw her flush and thought that she had done it. But she only shook her head again. "I've tried several times to do it like she wants, but she finally just started writing things down for me so that I can simply put them into the computer ledger. I realized after your family left that they got the wrong trash the other day. I noticed it when I took the can back to the office to shred the sheets she'd given me and figured out I'd given them to that woman. Mrs. Golden must have given them to you?"

"She did. And I can shred them if you'd like or bring them by. I know the importance of having things like that kept out of the trash." Another person went to the counter, and she stepped away.

Neal followed her but detoured to the alcove she'd come out of earlier. He saw the woman's back first. Then when she stood up, he was amazed at how tall she was. But it was when she turned to him that he nearly fell backwards.

"This is for employees only," she said. He nodded, unsure of himself for the first time in his life when it came to women. "That means, dickhead, that you're supposed to keep out."

"My name is Neal, not Dick." She frowned at him. He'd gotten she was insulting him. "Are you Rayne?"

"What is it you want? I'm sort of in the middle of something here, and I don't have time to shoot the shit with an illiterate person." She pointed to the large sign just behind him. "See, it basically says for you to stay the hell out."

He took a step toward her instead of backwards when she stepped toward him. He had the incredible urge to taste her and was just trying to figure out how to do that when someone came in behind him. He was pushed aside when a large man advanced to her.

"You fucking cunt, you called the cops on me." Neal stood up and reached for the man just as the woman did, and he had a moment of panic. Then nothing as her hand closed over his on the man's shoulder.

Chapter 3

Rayne hit Jeff Sanders in the face with all she had, and when he fell over unconscious, she stepped toward the younger man. She knew the second that their hands had touched, she was going to hurt him, but there was nothing she could do about it. She couldn't stop what was coming from her that quickly, even if she had wanted to. If he'd only left when she'd told him to, he'd be fine, and Sanders would be hurting all by himself.

Carefully, she stepped over him after making him more comfortable. Then she went out to the showroom to search for her mom. She was talking with another woman who had one full cart of her baskets and was putting more into a second one. It looked like she was going to have another good day. Her mom turned when she stepped close.

"I have a problem in the back." She looked around the showroom, then back at her. "A man came back, and I think—"

"Tall, good-looking man with light brown hair and a suit that looks as neat as a nice row of numbers?" She nodded at the other woman. "That would be my son. He said he needed to talk to you, that is, if you're Rayne Morrow. What did he do, piss you off by saying his name was Golden Golden?"

"Golden," Rayne asked. "Just how the hell many of you people are there? And yes, it would be him and Sanders too. He was coming back to...." Rayne took a deep breath, and the older woman started to laugh. She had started to say that Sanders had come back to get his pound of flesh but shut her mouth in time.

"I'll call my oldest. He'll come and collect his brother and Sanders if you let him. I believe my daughter Bronwyn wanted to speak to him anyway. Oh, and I have six sons and two very lovely daughters-in-law that I love more than them at times."

Rayne asked her mom if she could speak to her while the other woman pulled out her cell phone. "Sanders is back there, and when he wakes up, he's not going to be happy. I zapped him. The other guy, too, but that wasn't my fault."

"Oh, Rayne, why don't you press charges against that bully Sanders and then have him called to the carpet for not paying your bill? You could certainly use the money, and I wouldn't have to worry about you so much." She told her mom she'd pressed charges against him yesterday on her way home from him having his goon squad knock her around a bit. "Oh. Well, good then. But if he thinks that I'm going to allow him to harm you again, he's gonna have to tangle with me."

Mrs. Golden came up to her just as her mom went to cash someone out. She smiled at Rayne and nodded to the alcove. "Is he all right, or do you need to call an ambulance? His brothers are on their way here to see to the two of them. Though I'm sure not in the same way."

"If you know that Bronwyn woman, then you're aware of what kind of monster I am. I never wanted anyone to be hurt, but Sanders was coming at me. When I reached for him to shove him out, your son did as well, and I hurt him. For that, I'm sorry." Rayne looked back at her work area, then back at the woman. "I'd really like it if you people would just leave me alone. I never asked for your help, and as far as I'm concerned, when I missed that appointment, things between us was finished. Understand?"

"Oh, I understand what you're saying, but I don't agree with it." Before Rayne could tell the woman she didn't give a flying fuck what she believed, she continued. "As for the monster part? Not going to believe that any more than I can believe that I can fly. No one that makes things like this from nature can be called that horrid name. As for us people leaving you alone? I'm afraid that's not going to happen either. Last I heard from Bronwyn, she's planning to hire you to do the lobby for us, and I, for one, can see why."

"I can't do that job. I don't have the money for the upfront capital any longer." She flushed when she realized what she'd said. "I have some unforeseen hospital bills."

"I can see that you've taken a beating. Did someone I know do that to you?" She didn't answer, but she seemed to know anyway. "Sanders is a pain in the ass most days, but hitting a woman is about as low as it gets. How much have you healed yourself?"

"None. I can't do that. And why do you care?" Before she could answer, Bronwyn and a large man walked into the shop. She looked at Mrs. Golden, and she nodded. Rayne stepped up to them just as they started for the counter.

"He's in there. I didn't mean to hurt him, but I did it. I'll take full responsibility for it if you want to press charges." She started to turn when the man said her name.

"I want to know what Sanders did to you." His voice was hard and unforgiving. She took a step back when she felt his cat seem to slide along his skin. "I have a beef with him already."

"Good for you, but that doesn't concern me. If you're here to take your brother home, then go get him, but me and mine are not your concern." She turned in time to see his brother coming out of her work area.

He looked pale and seemed to be working hard at keeping upright. She moved when his brother went to help him stand. He moved toward her, and before she could figure out his intentions, he trapped her against the counter with his hands on either side of her.

"Ryland?" His brother, she supposed, moved forward. "Can you see to Sanders for me? This is my mate, and he hurt her."

Rayne heard her mom's sharp intake of breath and knew that she'd heard him. Before either of them could say a word, Ryland moved to her work area, and she heard him saying something to Sanders. She couldn't take her eyes off the man who had trapped her.

"You step back, or I'll shove you back. And this time, you won't be getting up for a little while." He smiled at her, and she found herself responding in a way that made her scared. "I'm not screwing around with you. I want you to back up and get the hell out of here."

"I'm not leaving until Sanders does, and since I'm reasonably sure that he's not leaving on his own two feet, I'm staying," he said. She put up her hand to push him away. "You can't hurt me. I'm your mate, and as such, you're not able to cause me any harm."

She fisted her hand and pointed a finger at him. "Fuck you," she said in a low voice just before she touched him again.

The power in her finger shot out at him and knocked him back. Before he could hit the floor, she lifted him up with the same finger and held him above her head. She walked him to the door and dropped him on the other side.

"I'm not now, nor will I ever be, anyone's mate. If you return here, I'll not be so kind about it." She turned to the rest of his family and glared. "You come here again, I'll have you arrested for trespassing and anything else I can think of. Then I'll—"

"Enough," her mom interrupted. Rayne looked at her. "I did not raise you to be a fool, and you know it. Tell them you're sorry right now, or so help me, I will get medieval all over your ass."

"But Mom, I—" Her mom simply put her hands on her hips, and Rayne shut up. She turned to the Goldens and noticed that Sanders was across Ryland's shoulder, still out. "I'm terribly sorry for the way I've acted. I can't really have you arrested, and I'm pretty sure that I need your business more than I need to keep you away. But I'm not going to be his mate."

"You already are, love, and you know how that works," her mom said, coming to stand next to her. "You all are welcome to finish whatever it is you need to do today. We can meet at my house to discuss this matter. I'll have dinner ready at six. And my daughter will be on her best behavior, won't you, Rayne?"

Rayne nodded and went back to finish the pots she had been working on. She was nearly finished with the first one when the man she'd tossed around like a rag doll came in and sat down. She decided to ignore him. It was that or pissing her mom off again.

~~~

Neal watched her work. He was amazed at the artistry she exhibited in her work on the different flowers she was arranging in the large crock. He noticed that there was another one sitting beside it, and he wondered if these were what the first man had been waiting on.

"I'm sorry." She didn't respond to him, but he smiled. "When I came here today, it was to offer you a partnership. Ryland said that it would be a good investment, and I have to agree with him. You have a good head on your shoulders, and you are damned good with your record keeping."

He saw her pause, but she didn't speak. He didn't care. Watching her was too much fun. When she bent to pick up a large bag of potting soil, he stood to take it from her when she told him to leave her alone.

"I've been doing this for a long time, and your help is not needed. In fact, don't you have somewhere else to be right now?" He told her no. He liked where she was. "I can't be tripping over you all day. Get the hell out of here."

He stood up and realized that he was bothering her, so he went out to the counter where Karin was ringing out his mom. They were talking about how to water the flowers that she was getting and what sort of sun they needed. He noticed that his brother was gone, but Bronwyn was still looking around. She had another cart of plants.

"I'll have to have Rayne get that for you, sir." Neal looked at Karin and the man standing to her left. "I can't lift things that heavy for very far. When she comes out, I'll have—"

"I can get it for him," Neal said. She looked at his suit, and he pulled off his jacket and tie. "Just tell me what it is, and I'll get it for him."

Karin looked a little nervous as she glanced at the area where her daughter was. He wanted to tell her that she and he would come to an agreement sooner or later, but he had a feeling she wouldn't believe that any more than he did. She was as stubborn as he'd heard she was.

Neal put the twenty bags of mulch on the two carts from the back storage area and rolled them up to the counter. Ryland was just coming in when he offered to help the man load it into his truck. He was dirty and sort of enjoying himself. Ryland helped him load them as the man paid.

"Is she really your mate or just hopeful thinking on your part?"

He told his brother both. "Yeah, I can see that. She's a little on the hardheaded side. And fucking amazing too. She lifted you up ten feet without touching you."

"I know, and dropped me from there too." He put the last bag in the truck and looked back at the shop. "I'm going to hang out here today. I think she could use the help, and I need...Ryland, I hate my job."

His brother nodded. "I know. Bronwyn said that she'd been feeling your resentment for some time."

He started to tell him he never resented his job when he realized that was it. He loved numbers. When they lined up in neat rows and added up to the correct sum, he was thrilled to death, but he felt that there had to be something out there that gave him more than that. He looked at the shop again.

"Do you suppose she'll let me have a job? I could work with her for a few days and come into the office a few days. I'm nearly burnt out, and this might have what I need." His brother nodded as they brought the empty carts back in. Karin asked him if he had some time to get another thing for her.

Ryland brought him in a shirt and a pair of tear-away pants to change into, then he and Bronwyn took his mom home along with her purchases. Neal parked Brock's truck as far from the front as he could, leaving the front spots for shoppers. He was pulling a large tree from the middle of a line of them when he smelled Rayne come up behind him.

"I thought I asked you to leave," she said. He handed the apple tree to the man and turned to Rayne, but before he could speak, she said, "You should have left over an hour ago, not getting in the way of customers."

"I've been helping the customers, not getting in their way, and your mom asked me to. Besides, you said to go away, not to leave.

I went away." She stiffened when he took a step toward her to go around. "I'm not going to touch you. Though I'm not sure how we being mates will work if I can't. But I'm sure there are ways."

He left her standing there as he went to help another customer lift a large container of flowers onto her trolley. He was watching the names of things as he put them out and helped tote them around. The ones he was helping with now were pansies. He thought they looked like happy little flowers. But damn, they were colorful.

He saw her a couple of more times over the next hour. She was helping customers as well. When her mom asked to speak to him, he walked to the counter where she was ringing out the customer. She smiled at him.

"I need to go and get us some lunch, but we've been so busy that I can't leave. Do you think you could run the register?" He looked at it and then at her. "Everything is marked with the prices, and when you can't find them, just use the intercom to call for Rayne. She has another three special projects to do, and the people need them today." He nodded.

How hard could it be?

Much harder than he'd ever thought it could be. First of all, he had no idea how to use the little wand thing. He'd called Rayne out twice when it refused to scan. Then she'd picked it up, and it read it like it was nothing. Then a man wanted to pay by check, as his credit card didn't scan. Rayne had told the man that she didn't accept checks because the bank wouldn't take them from her due to her status as a small business. He was sure it was more of a trust issue with the bank in that the customer's check might bounce, and she couldn't afford it. It was a nice way to say it, he thought. He'd heard that before from someone he'd met at the gym and decided he'd help her with that too. The man left but promised her he'd be back with cash. Neal thought he'd never return.

The fourth time she'd had to be called out, she'd huffed at him and told him to go back and get all the stuff she was working on and to bring it out where they were. He put everything on the cart and wheeled it out as she was telling a man that she wasn't available to go out with him, but thanks for asking. She glared at him when he growled.

"Behave. He asks me every time he comes in here. He has a wife and four kids. He comes in here once a month to buy her a planter. She kills them faster than I can pot them. But he stupidly loves her and keeps doing it."

"You don't believe in love?" he asked. She didn't answer him as she started to work on the project. He watched her between ringing out customers, and when he went to get something for someone, she manned the station. He thought they worked well together. When Karin returned, Rayne put her lunch aside and finished up while he devoured his.

"Tell me what to do, and I'll finish up while you eat." She told him no. "You have to be hungry. I know I was, and I've not been working nearly as hard as you were. Come on. I can shove a few posies in the dirt while you watch."

"Are you always this annoying?" He told her he was, but mostly when people were being too stubborn to eat when he could hear their belly growling. "Well, I don't need a fucking sitter."

"Then act like it," he said. She stomped away, and he followed her with her lunch. "You are by far the most pigheaded woman I've ever known. Eat the damned sandwich."

She snatched it from him and tore the wrapping open. He knew that her mom had made them lunch and had brought it back. His had been a thick roast beef sandwich with mayo, lettuce, and tomato. She'd also brought him some potato salad and a couple bottles of water. He sat down at the desk while she sat at the tiny table in the office.

"I'm not going to go away." She didn't answer him, but he'd come to realize she didn't answer when she wanted to argue. He thought she needed to argue more. He knew he did. "Do you know how much I want to press you against that table you're at and have my way with you?"

She dropped her fork, and he smiled. When she looked at him, he sobered up, deciding that she'd hurt him badly if she even thought he was making fun of her. When she glared, he decided to try another tactic, one less likely to get him murdered.

"Tell me about your business and where you see you in a few years." She took another bite of her sandwich, and he noticed that she had pasta salad, not potato. He wondered if she didn't like it or if her mom had brought different kinds of salad. Not that it really mattered, but even as full as he was, he thought he'd like to have a bowl of it as well.

"I just want to grow things and help others grow them too." He started to tell her that she had to want more. Then she shook her head. "No, that's not right. I want to work for myself and not...I can't work for other people, I guess. I don't play well, as my mother is fond of telling me. I guess you've figured that out as well. But my last job...I had to quit, kill someone for being just plain stupid, or at the very least be fired. My boss wanted more from me than I thought that his pissy checks covered. So my mom and I pooled our money, and we bought this place. I want to buy her out someday and support her, but she says she likes her job and figures that's good enough for her right now. She's the cook at the Casual Diner."

"My mom and I ate there this morning. It was really good." It was, too, and after thinking about the lunch he'd just eaten, he couldn't wait to eat there when Karin was there. "How long has she worked there?"

"Since my stepdad died. He's been gone for a few years. Mom was set up really well, no thanks to him. But she was bored, she said, and needed something more." He could relate to the being bored part. He'd been bored at his job for the past several years. He smiled at her when she stretched out her long legs. "He changed her when I was ten. He told me that he'd make me a wolf too when I got older, but he didn't live long enough. He was killed in a snowstorm when he came to pick my friend and me up from the mall. He didn't...he drove off a ravine and drowned in an iced-over pond he'd broken through."

"I'm sorry," he said. "Stan, that man who works for me, said he was a good man. He likes your mom too. I've been thinking that I need a change too. Something more than numbers, at least for a little while. Something that I can...I want to be outside in the sunlight and move around with other people. Help them when I can. I want to work for you." Rayne shook her head and stood up. "Wait, hear me out, please. I'm bored too. I've worked as an accountant for my entire adult life. I need a change, or I'm going to explode. I've really enjoyed working for you today."

"I can't help you. I don't have the money for someone to work for me, and I don't want you hanging around me like some sick puppy. I have to make this work. And I will. I don't want you here." He moved to stand in front of her, and she backed against the table. "Don't."

"How do I kiss you? How do I get to see if your skin is as soft as it looks and as tasty as I think it is?" Her breath hitched a little as he lowered his head to her shoulder and inhaled deeply. "You smell so good to me. Like warm sunny days and sex."

"You can't do this. I'm a monster, and I don't want you." He leaned in more and took a chance on running his tongue along her pounding pulse. She moaned as he pressed his mouth over it and nipped. "Please don't do this. I don't want you to get hurt."

He moved slowly as he suckled her flesh into his mouth and touched her arms. When nothing happened, he moved his hands up her elbows to her shoulders and wrapped around her. Her hands moved to his shoulders. He was sure she was going to push him away. Lifting his head, he looked at her mouth, and when she licked her lips, he groaned. The need to taste her was like a fix he needed. Lowering his head to her mouth, he was ready to taste what he was sure was paradise when something alerted him that they were about to have company. Her mom came around the corner.

Chapter 4

Karin's first instinct was to shove him away, but then she realized that he was not doing anything to her little girl that she didn't want. She made a mental note to be a little noisier when the young tiger was in the building or, for that matter, anywhere around her daughter. Smiling to herself, she went to the sink and turned on the water. She was washing her hands and thinking about the two of them together as a couple when she felt the tension in the room.

"I've locked up. All that needs to be finished is the two planters for Monday and then tomorrow's deliveries." She smiled bigger. "Oh, and I have to go to work in the morning for a little while. Not long, but I won't be able to be here when the Saturday morning rush comes in. I'm sorry."

"It'll be fine. Most of the people who come in know where you are anyway if you're not here. I can do it." Karin hoped that Neal would say he'd help. She nearly turned to hug him when he did.

"I have nothing going on at work on Saturdays. I'll be here." She turned then to nod when she saw her daughter was all the way across the room from him. They were going to need some help if this was ever going to come to mean she'd have grandchildren any time soon.

"No," Rayne said as she moved to the open doorway. "I don't want you coming around here anymore. I've told you that several times already. Just stay away from me and my shop."

Karin was sure that Rayne would have slammed out of the room had there been a door, but that was on the next budget. She looked at Neal as he stared at the door. The poor man looked like he wanted to strangle someone. She cleared her throat, and he turned to her.

"Is she always this stubborn, or is it just me?" Karin sat at the table and nodded to the chair across from her. "I don't know what to do. I'm afraid of touching her without her permission, and I don't have a clue…what is she, Mrs. Hull?"

She thought about telling him what she'd been telling people for years, but if he really was her mate—and she had no doubt now that he was—she felt he deserved the truth. Reaching under her shirt, she pulled out the medallion hanging on a gold chain and pulled it off.

"Do you know what this is?" He took it from her when she held it out. "It's very old, and you might not know the history behind it. But my family does, and now…well, I trust you with this, Neal. If you hurt her with this information, I'll kill you."

"It looks like some sort of faerie or something. Is that what she is? A faerie?" He shook his head. "No, they aren't real. I mean, right? They're not real."

He sounded so hopeful, but he needed to know if he was going to make her his. "Yes, she's a faerie, but not like you see in the movies. She doesn't have wings or any dust she sprinkles around. She just has her ability to do these amazing things that have gotten her into a little trouble in the past. And only a few of the things she's used on you."

He nodded. "She tossed me around like I was nothing. And

her touch…what is that? Some sort of protection shield?"

"Yes, but it's not part of what she is. That's her own doing. She won't let anyone get close to her because she doesn't trust anyone." Neal stood up to pace as she continued. "There was a man once, not long ago, who she fell in love with. He was a good man, not great, but good. They dated for several months before he asked her to marry him. It took her a long time to tell him yes because she had to work up the nerve to tell him what she could do."

"I take it he didn't take it well." She shook her head, knowing that was an understatement. "I'm not him or anything like him. I have my own secrets to keep from the outside world, and I'd die to protect her."

"That's what he said, too, up until she touched him without a shield." Karin stood up and patted him on the back. "I don't really have to work in the morning, but I'm giving you the chance to come in and try to work this out with her. But I'm not kidding you when I tell you that if you hurt her in any way, I will hunt you down and tear you apart."

He looked at her, and she could see that he believed her. He was bigger than her even as a human, and his cat would likely kill her as soon as she shifted with intent to harm him, but he knew she was serious. When he nodded, she started to tell him that she had other means than her wolf to hurt him, but then he spoke.

"If I hurt her in any way, I would gladly let you kill me." He moved to the door that led to the showroom. "I've spoken to my mom, and she would like for you to let her host this dinner tonight. She said that there are a great deal more of us than of you, and she'd very much like to have you two over to dinner."

"I can do that. Tell her that I'll bring desserts. I was going to have pork chops and trimming, but I like that better. I was wondering how to seat all of you." He nodded. "Neal, she's not going to be happy with either of us when she finds out I've told on her."

"I know. But I do thank you. And Mrs. Hull? I won't hurt her. I'll protect her with all that I am." He looked into the showroom and then back at her. "The man that hurt her, where is he?"

She smiled. "Please call me Karin, and he's dead."

~~~

Closing her eyes, Rayne let her power pour over her as she held the large container. She knew it was an unfair advantage she had over other florists and greenhouses in the area, but she had it and wanted things to work for her and her mom. She opened her eyes when she heard someone step into the room with her. Neal was standing there.

"That's how you have such lovely flowers. I like it. You give them a sort of jumpstart." He nodded, seemingly approving of what she was doing. "Do you do that to all your containers?"

"I thought you left." He shook his head and picked up one of her little plants. "You need to leave now. I have a lot of work to do and very little time to do it since my mother said I have to be at her house tonight."

"No, we're all going to my mom's house. She called and said she had more room for us all. Your mom is making some desserts to take over. Do you think they'll be anything like her food at the diner?" He put the flower in the dirt where she'd put hers only moments before. When he picked up the next two and did the same, she wanted to bash his head in.

"What the hell are you doing?" He grinned at her. "I won't have time to repot everything if you mess them up. Just back the hell off and let me do my job."

"I want to help," he said. "Either let me do this or I go to another part of the building and put some together to help you without your supervision." She huffed at him, and he laughed. "What's it going to be?"

She didn't answer him. He picked up the next plant and mimicked her every move until he got the large crock filled with flowers. She reached over to give it her power before she could think about it. They were on their fifth and sixth container when he spoke.

"I never got to kiss you." She almost fumbled the flower she was putting into the hole she'd made for it. "I really want to feel your mouth under mine when our bodies touch. Your skin tasted better than anything I've ever tasted before."

"You're not going to kiss me or anything else. What happened in the kitchen was a mistake, and it won't be repeated." She looked up at him when he snorted. "I'm serious. You can't be around me. I don't even know why I'm letting you be here now."

He stood up and stretched. Her body tightened. He was taller than most of the men she knew, and he was bigger too. She was sure that most accountants like he'd told her he was didn't have near the muscles that seemed to move along his forearms like they were alive. She dropped her head when he looked at her.

"Are you sure about that? From where I'm standing, I can see that you want me to kiss you. Maybe even do a little more than that." He raised his nose to the air. "I can smell you, your arousal. It's not strong yet, but I can change that if you…are you afraid of me and what I can make you feel, Rayne?"

"I most certainly am not afraid of you. If you remember correctly, I already showed you how unafraid I am of you." She snorted as she fixed the last two of the containers and moved to the area where she had some small herbs that she wanted to transplant. "I'm all finished now, so you should get the hell out of here."

She felt him follow behind her, but she didn't stop walking. He'd helped her get the larger items done, so she decided that she'd fix these for tomorrow. It was nice to have the extra time, but she wasn't going to get used to him or it. She didn't think he'd hang around if she kept giving him the cold shoulder. Or at least she hoped he wouldn't.

"These smell much better to me than the flowers." He picked up the thyme and held it to his nose. "Lemony. And…I don't know what the other is, but it's good."

She pinched one of the little leaves and watched his face as the scent hit his nose. He looked at her, shocked, and picked up another one and pinched it as she'd done. He did this several more times until he found the catnip. She wasn't sure what it would do to him, but when he sneezed three times in a row, she figured that big cats like him didn't like it like the little ones did. She laughed when he set it down and away from him. He looked at her.

"You should do that more often." She flushed. "Your laughter is like music to me, and I'd love to hear it more."

"I don't have a great deal to laugh about." She picked up the long wooden container and put parsley into the middle of it and then oregano on one end and the little thyme on the other. She did this to three more containers, grabbing herbs at random and filling them as he handed them to her. She looked up when there wasn't one held out to her.

"They're all full. What do you need to fill now?" She looked at the herb table and saw that working together, they'd filled nearly two dozen pots. They all looked like she'd given them her power too. She looked at him, suddenly afraid that she'd touched him with it.

"I was careful not to touch you when I saw what you were doing. But it was fascinating to see you work without any sort of restrictions. Did you know that your eyes change from brown to almost clear when you do that?" He moved around the table, picking up the empty bags of potting soil and brushing the extra dirt they'd spilled into a bucket. "I'm assuming that's why you do your work behind that wall over there. So no one will see you."

"They'd freak out," she said. He nodded. "Why are you doing this? I've told you several times I want you to leave, but you keep hanging around. Why?"

"I've thought about nothing but you since I've figured out who you are to me." She shook her head, and he nodded as he sat the bucket on the table. "But I have. And you can deny it all you want, but you're my mate, Rayne. No amount of you shaking your head or trying to deny that will change a thing."

"I don't need you." He smiled at her as he took a step toward her. "And I don't want a mate. I have enough problems on my own without a male coming around thinking he can order me around like I'm his property."

"I have property, and I'd never put you in the same category as that is. It's a thing to me. You are not. And I have possessions, too, but you'll never be that to me either. I have too much respect for you to do that. My mate is what I want and need from you, a partner that works and lives beside me, not someone for me to have hanging on my arm. I want you to be a part of me and not lose yourself in me."

"I don't want any of that. You should find someone else." He shook his head, and she knew that he was going to tell her that he couldn't, not now. "I can't be anything to you, Neal. You have to realize that."

He had backed her into a wall, and she wanted to run. But he was so close to her that she could see the different colors in his eyes, browns and golds along with greens and blues. When he moaned her name, she realized she'd licked her lips and watched as he lowered his head.

"I want you to kiss me, Rayne. Blend my mouth with yours and kiss me." She wanted to tell him no, but her body was screaming at her to at least try to kiss him. She touched her mouth to his and felt his warmth. His breath moved over her cheeks as he exhaled softly. She wanted to touch him with her fingers. Shaking, she lifted her hand to his face and ran her finger along his cheek to his throat as her mouth was hovering above his.

"If I kiss you...when I kiss you, I want to give you some of me. You'll see then why this won't work." He nodded and ran his tongue over her parted lips. "You should hold onto something."

His arms wrapped around her, and she felt his body become flush with hers. As her mouth covered his, she let just a little of the power she knew she had go and knew when he'd felt it too. He stiffened, but before she could pull back, he rocked her into the wall and groaned loudly against her mouth.

A kaleidoscope of color danced beneath her closed eyes. When he lifted her up to his hard cock, she curled her fingers into his hair and pulled him tighter to her. Her legs wrapped around his hips, and he held her closer to him. When he lifted his head and looked at her, she saw his hunger and his need. Before she could decide what to do, he nuzzled her neck and suckled her pulse into his mouth as he'd done in the kitchen.

"I want you." She wanted to nod, to beg him to take her, but he lifted his head again. "But I can't. Not like this. You still don't trust me, and as much as I'd like to mark you as mine, I won't do that now either. As I said, I have entirely too much respect for you to do that."

He sat her feet down on the floor and took a small step back. Before she could unwind her arms from him, he leaned in and kissed her again. His tongue danced along hers several times as she chased his with hers. When he lifted his head this time, he took her lower lip into his mouth and nibbled on it before letting it go. They were both breathing hard.

"Christ, do you have any idea how much I want to drop to my knees right now and drink from you?" He leaned his forehead to hers, and she heard him chuckle slightly. "I'm not going to survive this, am I?"

Rayne pushed him away and moved to the light panels along the wall. She didn't care if he followed her or not. She just needed to get away from him. She'd not rejected him; he'd done that all on his own. When the last light was out, she moved to the front of the shop and turned the handle to close off the office, only to feel him put this hand over hers.

"Why can I touch you?" His breath was warm on her neck. "Before, when we touched, it was painful. Why not now?"

She shook her head, not able to answer him right away because she knew the answer as well as he did. He was her mate. She turned to him and looked him in the eye.

"Men have done nothing but take and take from me since I was a child. A neighbor found out that I could make our tree grow fruits better than his, and he tried to poison our tree, killing some of the animals that lived in it. Another man decided that having me as his wife was going to be to his advantage because he thought, because if I could protect his little dog from his wrath that I could keep him safe when he sold his drugs." She tried to turn away, but he held her, and she told him what hurt her the most. "Then there was a man that I really and truly loved. And I tried to tell him I was different, that before I'd marry him, he had to know the real me, the person I hide from everyone. He said he could handle it, that loving me was all he could think above anything else. That whatever it was didn't matter to him. But it did."

He pulled her chin up when she dropped it, trying her best to hide the truth even from him. "What did he do? How did he hurt you?"

When she pulled away from him this time, he let her but only so far. Then he moved in closer and stood near her so closely that she could feel his heat at her back. Looking out into the dark parking lot to her right, she saw a car and assumed it was his. She told him what she'd never even told her mom.

"He sat on the couch and waited for me to prove whatever it was that I felt I had to do. He hadn't even wanted to believe the small stuff. I'd shown him plenty of times before things that I never mentioned to him, but he had to notice. But when I let go, he sat there so quietly afterwards that I was afraid. And when he stood up and walked to me, I thought maybe I'd been wrong about him, that he would...I don't know. Continue to love me. But he hit me. Drew back his fist and slammed it into my face. When I looked up at him, he stood over me and screamed at me to get up. To stand up and tell him the lies again so that he could knock them out of me. I was so confused that I stood up."

She thought about that night so often that she could see it like it was a movie in her mind. When she'd stood up, he'd grabbed her around the throat and started to squeeze her. As she clawed at his hands to make him let her go, he smiled at her. A smile that she'd never forget as long as she lived. A smile that told her that the man she'd come to love had been nothing more than a monster hiding behind a façade. And he was going to kill her.

But she'd let herself go limp. And when he had shaken her, she felt her power run up her arms to her hands as darkness started to take her. Lack of air had her losing her grip as well. When she touched him, she felt him fling her away...and then nothing at all.

"You killed him." She'd forgotten he was there and hadn't realized that she'd spoken aloud until he asked her. She supposed he didn't ask her, really, but she answered anyway.

"Yes. Someone must have heard the fight and called the police. My mom came to the apartment a few minutes after they had arrived. She told the police I was breaking it off with him, and he must have gotten pissed." She turned when he pulled her around to him. "My mom knew that I had probably killed Jeff, but she had never asked. I think I might have scared her a little, but she never said anything more about him, ever."

"You didn't tell her what happened?" She shook her head. "And what did the police say? I'm assuming you didn't go to jail."

"For a little while, about four days. One of the officers kept me informed and told me that they were investigating some other crimes. They knew him from some other relationships, I guess. He'd been an abusive bastard all his life, but they had thought when there hadn't been any calls for a while that...." She pushed him away. "It doesn't matter, Neal. We can't be together. I won't have another man hurt me."

He didn't say anything as they moved toward the exit. She had a feeling that it was far from over with him. He'd argue because it seemed to be something he enjoyed doing, but she was going to stand firm on this. Neal had to understand that she was not going to be his little mate, and there was no way she was going to have sex with him. No matter how much she...he wanted it.

When she stepped into the night, she knew they weren't alone seconds before someone stepped in front of them. She had about half a second to protect them both before the shots were fired.

Chapter 5

"No, I didn't know who he was." Neal wanted to go to the police officer and knock him on the head, but Ryland held him back. He said to see how Rayne handled the cop. That's what he was afraid of, that she'd handle him like she'd done the man who'd shot at them.

"Did he say anything? Or tell you why he wanted to kill you?" She shook her head and told him he hadn't said a word. "How about if he told you who hired him?"

"If he hadn't said a word, then I'm reasonably sure that he didn't tell me who hired him. And for the record, that would also cover him not telling me why he wanted to kill me." Neal watched her glare at the cop as he started to ask her something else. "You ask me again if he said anything, and I won't be responsible for what I do to you."

Ryland laughed and changed it to a cough when Rayne glared at him. Neal had had enough and went around his brother and to Rayne. He looked at the cop, who had been the first on the scene and had been driving them both crazy since.

"Have you seen to her wound yet?" He shook his head and then looked at her. "Then I would suggest that you do that right now. I think she's answered your questions enough times that you should be able to write a book about it."

He saw his brother coming toward them and could have leapt for joy. Alistair would settle this, and they could go home. Neal, for one, was tired of standing around while they tried to figure this out. Alistair shook his hand and started to put out his hand to Rayne but pulled back. So he'd been warned too. It might have been funny if he wasn't already so pissed off that he might have hurt someone himself.

"I'm their attorney, Alistair Golden, and I'm here to see what kind of idiot makes a woman who's been shot nearly thirty minutes ago still sit here bleeding. Is this the way we treat our victims? I certainly hope to Christ not." Alistair yelled for someone in charge, and the police captain came to where they were standing almost immediately. Alistair asked him the same thing.

"We offered her medical assistance, and she said she couldn't afford it. So, we've been asking her questions. She said she didn't have a lawyer, not that we said she needed one. Looks like a clear case of self-defense if you ask me." All of them looked at the body and then at Bronwyn, who simply shrugged. "Looks to me like he was intending to rob them, and well, as you can see, they took care of it."

Not what happened at all, and Neal was pretty sure that anyone who Bronwyn hadn't "adjusted" to see things this way could tell. The man had been killed, and that was all that was correct in the statement. When the police said they could go, he had to remind Rayne that her mom was at his mom's home, or she would have gone to her own place. The ride in Ryland's car to the house was made mostly in silence. Bronwyn was the only one talking, and she was doing it a mile a minute.

"Mom had the cook make something that could wait, not

knowing when you shut your shop down." Bronwyn looked at him and smiled. "It's been a while since we've had a big dinner at your mom's house. She said she wanted to do it more often, especially after the—"

"Pull over. I'm sick." Ryland jerked the wheel to the side of the road and stopped the car just as Rayne leapt from it. When Neal made to follow her, Bronwyn stopped him.

"She might need a minute or two. Apparently, this happens when she's really upset, and I'd say this qualifies." She nodded after a few more minutes. "Go to her, but, Neal, you might want to tread lightly. She's really close to the edge right now."

He nodded and moved out of the car to where he could see her outline. Bronwyn handed him a few things as he was slipping out, and he put them in his pockets. He walked up beside her but didn't touch her for fear of upsetting her. She looked at him when he handed her his handkerchief.

"I killed that man, and there was no way that anyone looking at him would see anything but murder." He took her hand and held it, just glad for the contact. "What did she do to them? Fuck with their mind so they'd see it her way?"

"Pretty much, I would say. She's really good at it and…." He closed his mouth on the rest of that thought. He'd been about to tell her that Bronwyn could do all sorts of things to one's mind but thought that might be a little too much.

"He was going to kill me. He was sent there to kill me, and he was being paid to do so." He looked back at the car and wondered if Bronwyn had gotten who had sent him to kill Rayne and almost missed what Rayne said. "I would very much appreciate it if you would tell your family that—"

He cut her off with his mouth. He didn't want to hear anything she might say about them not seeing each other, about her not wanting him to come to work with her. He wanted to be with her. He wasn't stupid enough to think he could protect her by being there because she'd proved tonight that she could do that without him. He deepened the kiss and pulled her closer to his body. She moaned when he cupped her ass and rocked into her hard.

"Please don't do this." He licked a path along her throat and felt her body shiver. He wanted to bite her, wanted to mark her, but held off. He wasn't sure what would happen if he did, and as much as he thought about taking the chance, he did want her to trust him. Lifting his head, he kissed her mouth tenderly and held her under his chin.

"I don't want to talk about you not wanting me around you, please. We have something going here, and I don't want to fuck it up by upsetting you anymore. You'll come to our house; we'll eat, then if you're not too tired, we'll talk. But not right now."

She nodded. "Neal, this won't change my mind. You and I aren't going to happen. I don't want a mate."

He didn't point out that she already had one but led her back to the car. Bronwyn smiled at them both from the front seat and then turned to Ryland. He nearly pulled into moving traffic when she told him she thought she was in labor.

Rayne reached for her hand, and Bronwyn took it. He could see the difference in her face immediately. It took him a few seconds to realize they were still headed to his mom's house and not the clinic. He started to say something when Ryland tossed him his cell.

"Call Sindy. Tell her it's game time and to come to the house. And Mom. Don't forget to call Mom because—" Rayne touched him as well with her other hand. "Christ."

"I want you to pull over and slide to the back seat. You're going to let your brother drive before you fucking get us all killed. And stop barking orders. You sound like my stepfather." She looked at Neal. "Drive, and don't make me have to smack you to keep you in line either."

He nodded, and as soon as the car stopped, he rolled out and switched places with Ryland. When Rayne told him to wait a minute, he simply sat at the wheel and waited for her to tell him what to do. She looked at him in the rearview mirror as she sat behind him.

"Neal, I need you to call for an ambulance to come to us. Tell them what's going on, that Mrs. Golden is having contractions about two minutes apart." He nodded, suddenly very calm because she was. "Ryland, I want you to go around the car and lift your wife up and take her to the side of the road. There's a picnic table over there, and we'll use it."

"She's not having a baby on the side of the road." Rayne grabbed him by the hair so quickly that she had him moving back when he snapped at her.

"Now you listen here, you overgrown bossy prick, that baby is coming. We can have it right here in the car where I might pull the wrong part from the wrong person." She looked down at his groin, then at Ryland's face again. "Or you fucking do what I tell you and take her over there. Now, big boy, or I carry her myself."

Bronwyn laughed. "I like you, kid. If you promise to do this again to Ryland when he gets out of hand, I'll be your slave for life."

"I don't want a slave. I just want to be left alone. And when he lifts you out of here, you're going to lose my hand. The pain is going to hit you like a knife until I can get to you again. Understand?" Bronwyn nodded and took a deep breath. When Ryland put his hands under her to lift her, Bronwyn let her go with a cry. She looked at Rayne and told her to hurry.

By the time Neal had made the calls, Rayne had Bronwyn on the table, and her jeans pulled off. He tried to stay back, but Ryland grabbed him. He didn't think he'd ever seen his brother look so terrified in all his life.

"She's having the baby. I don't know what to do." Neal wanted to laugh; his big brother was falling apart, but then sobered when he realized that when he and Rayne had a child, he was going to need someone too.

"Do you have the baby bag in the car?" Ryland nodded. "Get it and anything else you might find that will cover them up when the baby comes. And water, if there is any water, then bring it too."

He went to stand next to Rayne and asked her what she needed. "Open that first-aid kit and find me some scissors and some string. If you can find some wet wipes, that'll be great too." She was still calm, but he knew she was nervous. Her hands were shaking when he handed her a half dozen wipes.

Bronwyn screamed, and Ryland paled. The man looked like he was going to drop over when Rayne barked at him to help his wife breathe. Neal watched her as she moved from one task to the next, keeping the mother and father calm while making sure that everything was going well with the baby. When Bronwyn told her she needed to push, it only took three really straining pushes, and there was the baby.

The police pulled up just as Rayne handed the baby to Ryland. She had wrapped her up in one of the baby blankets that had been packed in the diaper bag. She finished up with Bronwyn as the first officer assisted. By the time the ambulance pulled up, Bronwyn and Ryland were holding their daughter, and the police officer was taking a statement. This man seemed to know just when to back off.

The medic said that everything was perfect and offered

Bronwyn something for pain. She refused him with a smile and told him she'd needed it a few minutes ago, but for now, she had all she needed. As they loaded her up, he started for his brother's car to follow them in when Ryland spoke to him.

"She saved her." He looked at Rayne as she leaned her head against the window. *"And she's a bossy little thing that needs to know her...I won't be able to ever repay her for what she's done for me and my family."*

"I don't think she'll see it that way, but I'll let her know. She wants me to take her home before I drop off your car. You want to see her, right?" His brother laughed. *"I mean, if I take her home, she won't get to hear from you how much you appreciate her being here for you tonight."*

"Tell her that I need her here for me. That I have something for her." His brother laughed. *"She's going to be pissed when she finds out what I've done today. But now I'm glad I did it. She'll not have to worry about Sanders again."*

"Please tell me you didn't kill him." Ryland laughed again. *"I mean, I appreciate the gesture and all, but I think that there's been enough killing today, don't you?"*

"Yes, I do, and I didn't kill him as much as I'd like to do that and bury him in a trash bag and put him six feet under. But he will pay her what he owes her. As will the other accounts that are past due. By the way, she's going to need an accountant. You know of anyone who might want the job?"

Christ, he hoped he did but wasn't sure with her. She was going to be pissed enough that his brother had helped her, and he hated to think what she'd say when she found out that he was her accountant too. He told his brother he'd see him soon and closed the connection. Neal looked over at Rayne and noticed she was asleep. He pulled out his phone and called his mom.

"Mom, can you make sure that Karin comes with you to the hospital." He knew that she was on her way in as Ryland had sent pictures to them all as soon as his daughter was born. "I think that Rayne might need her."

"She's with me, and we're stopping to pick her up something to eat too. Karin said she'll be starved." He heard someone speaking and waited. "Karin wants to know if Rayne helped with Bronwyn's pain."

"Yes. Why? Does that make a difference in what she needs? I can stop and get whatever she needs. I'm nearly to the hospital, but I can make a detour."

"She said something sweet. It doesn't matter what it is as long as it's sweet. She said sweet tea works the best, and she likes it." He nodded and pulled into the first fast-food restaurant he saw. "She also said that she was going to be cold when she woke up. That you should see if she'll let you hold her to keep her from shaking too hard."

That scared him a little, but he ordered three large teas and told her he'd see her there. Putting the drinks in all the holders, he said her name softly until she woke, and he handed her the first glass. By the time they were at the hospital, she was finishing the last one, and the shaking had begun.

~~~

She wanted to pull away from his heat, but he felt too good to her just now. She was freezing and shaking so hard that her teeth hurt, and her back was killing her. She tried to get closer without crawling into his lap, but he pulled her into it anyway. And she didn't have the energy to waste in trying to get him to put her back on the seat and to leave her alone. Not that she wanted him to right now, but she thought it was for the best if he did.

"I've got you." He'd been saying that since he'd pulled her to him, and she wondered what he meant. "Your mom said that she has you some food, and as soon as you're better, I'll take you in to get it."

"No. I can't. I have to go home and take a shower." She nuzzled into his neck, liking the way he smelled and realized what she was doing. Before she could pull away, he cupped the back of her head and held her there.

"I'm going to babble. I don't know if you find that to be irritating or not, but I can't hold you like this without thinking of all the things I'd like to do to you right now. So, let me think." He shifted on the seat, and she moved as well. His cock was hard beneath her, and she couldn't stop the moan that spilled from her mouth. The next thing she knew, she was licking his skin.

He tasted of sweat and a slight bitterness of his cologne. She inhaled deeply against his skin and could almost feel the warmth of the sun as it beat down on them. And he smelled of the spray of the water from some ocean. When he curled his fingers in her hair and lifted her head up, she realized she was no longer shaking but was very warm.

"You keep that up, and I'm not going to be able to keep from laying you back across this seat and taking you." She wasn't sure that wasn't a bad idea right now, but before she could tell him, he lowered his head and kissed her.

Rayne didn't have a lot of experience in kissing. The one and only man she'd kissed had been Jeff, and she was positive that he'd never kissed her like Neal was doing right now. When he cupped her breast, she put her hand over his to stop him, but it turned into her helping him massage her. Nothing had felt this good to her, and she found that she wanted more, a great deal more.

"I want to see you." His breath was husky and warm against her neck as he spoke. "I just need to see what delights you have beneath this shirt."

He lifted her tee-shirt up, and his fingers slid under her bra. When she felt him graze his knuckles against her nipple, she moaned. And her nipple tightened under his thumb and finger so much so that she felt a slight pain. Then his mouth was there. And every thought in her mind seemed to center on what he was making her feel.

"Please." Begging him to give her more had her moan then another. She wanted him, not just him but anything and everything he could offer her. When he lifted his head, she watched his eyes as she felt his hand move down her ribs to her belly and then to the top of her pants. She was panting by the time he moved down her hip to her thigh, then just at the apex of her leg. Nodding at him, giving him the permission he seemed to need to continue, he cupped her sex, and she nearly came up off him.

His mouth was everywhere at once. Her throat, her mouth, he was licking a path along the curve of her right breast, then the left. Each time he passed over her nipple, he would suckle it hard and bite while his fingers were dancing hard against her clit.

"I need to taste more of you." He shifted her around so that she was lying under the steering wheel, and he was moving to the floor of the car. In what seemed like seconds, her pants were off, and he was nibbling a path from her ankle to her knee. And the closer he got to her pussy, she felt herself get wetter and wetter.

"Neal, this is way beyond what we should be doing in a public parking lot." He grinned at her over her knees. "You should maybe not be—"

She screamed. There was no help for it. He'd slid his finger under her panties and into her. At the same time, he nipped hard at her cloth-covered clit. Her climax rolled through her as a sudden storm did in the heightened summer. And in the wake of the storm, like her body after her first real climax, she was shaken and wet. As soon as she felt her world center again, he suckled her into his mouth and commanded her to come again.

Her body was still hurling through another climax when he sat up between her legs on the seat. Her body went into overdrive as he freed his cock and fisted himself. She sat up and reached for him. He helped her wrap her hand around him as she moved to his mouth to taste her on his mouth and lips. Moaning, she moved closer to him and felt his heat as it seemed to call to her.

His cock was hard and soft at the same time. Silky and smooth, his cock felt slick in her hand, and she looked down to see the stream of precum sliding over their hands. When she leaned down to lick it off him, he pulled her up and looked at her.

"I want to bury myself in you." His hand tightened around hers as she ran her thumb over the tip of him. "Christ, I need to come right now. I want to come in you."

Moving up on her knees, she wasn't really sure what to do, and he helped her with that. He lifted her up over him, and she straddled his thighs. She looked at him as he held her hips, still hovering just above him.

"If I come in you, and I want to with every part of me, that will mark you as mine, Rayne. If I come on you, it will do the same. Even if you take me in your mouth right now and I come down your throat, I'm going to claim you. Anything we do from this point on is going to mark you as mine." She watched him as she curled her hands tighter into his shoulders. "What do you want?"

He was leaving it up to her. Marking her would do just what she didn't want, but not having him inside of her or even on her wasn't really an option at this point. She needed him as badly as he apparently needed her.

"I want you." He nodded once and moved her so that he was

just at her entrance. She came down on his cock so quickly and so fully that she cried out again from the sharp pain. He held her to him as she buried her face in his shoulder and tried not to cry.

"I'm so sorry, baby. I'm so sorry. I didn't think you'd be a virgin. I'm such an ass. A fool, I'm a fool, and I'll never forgive myself for hurting you." Rolling her hips, she lifted her head to look at him and felt her movement through his entire body. "Don't move."

His command was short-lived when she moved again over him. His fingers tightened on her hips, and she knew that she had a power over him that few would ever have over this man. As soon as she moved again, this time riding him, he took her bare breast into his mouth and nipped. Wrapping her hands around him, she felt her climax racing toward her with such speed that she knew that if he didn't come with her this time, she was going to pass out, and he'd be left to his own.

As soon as she arched her back and cried out again, his tongue moved along her breast to her throat. She knew he was going to bite her and tilted her head to the side to give him whatever he wanted of her. The moment he sank his sharp canines into her, she felt him roar against her flesh, his cum splash deep within her, and her entire body tightened around him as she fell over the edge of darkness. *Christ, I have a mate* was her last thought.

Chapter 6

Neal held her over him and tried to wrap his mind around what they'd just done in his brother's car. If Ryland thought he was getting it back after this, he was fucking insane. Smiling to himself, he licked the wound closed at her throat and pulled her to his body as he reached for his shirt to cover her with. Looking around the big lot, he realized that they were lucky no one had seen them.

Holding her as gently as he could, he tried to find his cell phone and finally gave up. He reached for his brother and told him that they weren't coming inside. He also told him he was going to buy his car.

"I'm not going to sell you my car, Neal. What the fuck did you do to it that would think I'd do such a stupid thing?" He told him that he'd mated with Rayne in it. *"That's just gross. What the fuck, man, you couldn't find a bed or a hotel?"*

"No, there wasn't any time. I'm sure you've felt that before too." He tightened his arms around her and sighed. *"I never knew it would be like this. I mean, I've heard you and Bronwyn talk about how it felt, but...."*

"I know. It's hard to describe. She's going to change you in

ways you've never dreamed of before. And having a child with her? There is no greater feeling in the world than that. My daughter is everything to me right now and more. I don't…I'm not sure that this can covey what I'm feeling to you right now, but Christ, Neal, I'm a father."

Neal laughed and told his brother that he loved him. *"I still need to buy your car. I think that having this thing around will help me too. All I have is that little two-door, and as I'm working two jobs now, I think you owe me. Besides, this thing can haul a lot of kids."*

After a few more comments about the car and neither of them giving up on the fact that they weren't giving in, they closed their connection. Neal wasn't sure how to get Rayne home when he couldn't seem to stop touching her. When she stirred in his arms, he looked down at her face and smiled.

"How are you feeling?" She nodded and stretched, and his cock moved inside of her. She stared at him for a few seconds before she moved her hips. "You shouldn't do that right now, love. If you do, then we're not going to leave this parking place for a long while yet, and I see a couple coming toward us."

She turned to look, and he took her nipple in his mouth and nipped. She rolled her hips again without turning, and he moaned. When she turned back to him, he saw devilment in her eyes.

"Can you make me come right now? If you do, when you take me home, I'll suck on your cock. I want to taste you—" He reached between her legs and pinched her clit, and covered her mouth with his hand. As she screamed out her release, he held her over him as his cock filled again. As soon as the couple moved past them, he rolled her to the seat and plowed into her. She wrapped her legs around him, and he took her mouth as hard as he did her pussy.

"Come with me again." He leaned down and bit her earlobe.

"Come, Rayne, and I'll take you to my house and fuck you all night long."

Her body arched up, and he felt her milk him. When she buried her nose in his neck, he wanted to beg her to bite him, but he never got the chance. As soon as he felt her teeth graze his shoulder, he felt his cock spew, his balls so tight that he roared loudly. When she bit him and sank her teeth into his muscle, he knew the moment she'd broken skin. Their connection was so amazing that he felt his world pinpoint to nothing but darkness for several seconds before he felt his body jerk again through a hard climax.

Neal dropped over her, having nowhere else to go. When she giggled at him, he lifted his head with the last of his strength and kissed her on the mouth. She smiled at him.

"You should know that you're very heavy." He nodded but didn't move off her. "And you should know that I think I have your pant leg on mine."

He looked down her body and could see that her leg was tangled up in his pants and that they'd managed to tear them. He looked back up at her and smiled.

"I guess we're going to my house after all. I don't seem to have any pants for work tomorrow, and you know what my new boss will think about me being half naked at work." She nodded. "What time do we have to be there anyway?"

"*I* have to be in at six. I have to finish up some planters that are going to be picked up first thing. But we don't open until nine. If you take me home, you can come back at around eight-thirty, and you won't have to—"

He shifted and sat up, leaving her laying there all delicious and wonderfully sated looking. "I'm not sleeping without you. Now that I've had a taste of you, I'm not ready to give you up so soon. If ever."

She looked at him as he adjusted his pants. He could feel her now, all her emotions, and he wondered at them as she went from sated mate to upset one, then fear. He handed her her pants and watched her pull them on.

"Tell me what you're thinking, Rayne. I can feel that you're upset, but not about what." She pulled her shirt over her head, not bothering with her bra. He shoved it in his pocket and watched as she struggled with her shoes. Finally, he reached his own and put his hand over hers. "Tell me."

"I don't want a boss." He sat back at the venom in her voice. "I could do all sorts of things before you came along, and I'm pretty sure I can still do them now that you've marked me. And you have, haven't you? And I have you."

He nodded, not sure what to say to her. He was about to argue with her when he felt Bronwyn touch his mind. She asked him if he was all right.

"No, I'm not fucking all right. She's like this pendulum swinging back and forth. Her moods are so quick I can hardly keep up with them." He felt her laughter. *"This is not fucking funny. I'm not the heavy here."*

"Sure you are. You're strong and confident, and she's not. For all her power and magic, she's still been hurt by others in ways you'll never understand. What do you expect her to do when you start to act like a Golden? You should ask her what she wants from you." He snorted at her. *"Then don't. I like her despite the fact that she's mated to you. And if she has to kill you, I'll take her side."*

"All I did was tell her that we'd have to go back to my house because I don't have any pants to wear to work in the morning." He flushed when he realized what he'd said to his sister-in-law. *"She and I are mates."*

"I gathered that. But did you ask her, or did you command

her? You might want to ask next time. She's pretty independent and will kick your ass. And about this working for her, again, did you ask or tell her? I'm telling you right now, Neal, she's not going to be a push-over just because you had great sex with her in the front seat of a car in a busy parking lot. I don't suppose it occurred to you that she could be embarrassed about what the two of you just did. Was she a virgin?"

He felt his face heat and wondered why he even thought he could talk to this woman or, for that matter, why did she fucking know when he was having problems? Did she have her radar set on him all the time?

"No, but because of what I am to you and the fact that I'm a little more...in tune to you than Ryland, I can feel when you're upset. And it's not just you I have radar on, but all of you. And now Rayne as well, thanks to the fact that she marked you as well." She laughed. *"So, buck up and tell her you're sorry and take her home with you. But you'd better behave. What she doesn't do to you, I most certainly will."*

He looked over at Rayne when the door opened. He watched her walk around the car and to where he was sitting. She jerked open the door.

"I can't drive this thing, and I want to go home. My home, right fucking now. I'm tired, and I'm hungry, and I'm sore." She shifted on her feet, and he realized that this was what Bronwyn was talking about. He'd hurt her but not really physically, though he was sure he'd done that as well. He heard her say thank you and told her he loved her just before he closed their connection.

"I'm sorry." Rayne raised a brow at him, and he got out of the SUV and stood before her, wanting to touch her but afraid to. "I'm an asshole and a jerk. I shouldn't have taken you so hard, and I certainly should have waited until we were in a more private place as well as a more comfortable setting before doing this to you."

"I wanted it too." She looked away, and he saw the set of her mouth and knew she was still pissed. At him or her or the two of them, he wasn't sure, but she was mad. "I could have said no plenty of times. You even asked me before we…." She didn't finish, so he did.

"Before I fucked you like an animal." He lifted his hand when she started to speak. "I did too. You enjoyed it, yes, but I could have been a little more…gentle with you."

She looked back at him as they both stood there. "I want to go home, not to your home but to mine. I think…I know that I wanted you, too, but this is moving really fast, and I need to slow down."

He nodded. "I understand, but would it be all right if I went by my house and picked up something for in the morning and stayed with you? I promise I'll sleep on the couch if you want. But after that man tried to hurt you and now making love with you…I need to be near you."

"I don't own a couch. All I have is a table and one chair, a bed with a single dresser and a closet-sized bathroom. I'm not set up for a man your size." She flushed. "My bed, it's big but not like you. How tall are you?"

"Six foot five inches. I'm actually shorter than two of my brothers. Jules is taller by an inch, and Alistair is an inch taller than him." He took her hand and kissed it. "How about a large pizza after I pick up some clothes. And I promise to sleep with you without taking up all your bed."

He watched her struggle with his request. What he really wanted to do was take her home, run a warm bath for them both, and then put her to bed. He thought about the hot tub off his room that hadn't been used in years. He had actually considered getting rid of it and decided to have Carl, his butler, get it cleaned and set up for them. Neal could see taking her in it and reached for the door handle to help her in the car before he embarrassed both of them and dropped to his knees and begged her to let him drink from her again.

"I don't care for pizza when I'm this hungry. Would you mind if we went to the diner? My mom has been raving about this new burger she's been making. I'll treat if you want."

It was on the tip of his tongue to tell her he would pay, but he snapped the thought down. He nodded instead and told her that would be payment enough for working today. He went to the other side of the car after helping her in and slid in under the steering wheel. His phone rang just as he was pulling into traffic, and he had Rayne answer it. It was for her anyway.

~~~

"Oh darling, she's just beautiful." Rayne smiled at her mom. "She looks just like her mother and already has the temperament of her father. You did a great job."

"I had help. I'm going to Neal's house. Then we're going to get something to eat at the diner. We've...." She wasn't sure what to tell her mom, but she understood.

"Congratulations are in order then. I'm happy for you, dear. He's a good man and has a wonderful family. I like them a great deal." Her mom laughed. "I understand that you have an envelope here to pick up. It seems that they've helped you get your money from Sanders. I'm glad. I think you're going to need to add on to your house soon."

"Money?" She glanced at Neal and realized he knew about it too. "I see. And what else has the Golden family done for me that no one bothered to tell me about?"

"I think Bronwyn wanted to tell you, but you are going to do the lobby for them. The exposure for your business will benefit from it as well." Her mom went on as Rayne tried to digest what she had said. The project was hers? How the hell did that happen? Then she realized that it was because of the baby.

"Mom, do you think I could speak to either Ryland or Bronwyn? I want to talk to them about the project." She told her that she'd left them both at the hospital, but Ryland was going to see her in the morning.

"He said that he has some other things he wants to discuss with you about other projects. And he said that he's put out the word what a great job you've done as well as saving his wife and child."

She was on a runaway freight train with no conductor. She took several deep breaths as her mom continued on about how she was able to come in tomorrow, after all, and that she was excited to see the new pots that were due to arrive on the truck in the morning. She'd forgotten about that. She told her mom that she loved her and closed the phone. She sat looking out the window at nothing for a few minutes before she realized that Neal was speaking to her. She turned on him.

"Did you know? About the money? Did you know that your brother was going to get it for me? What did he do? Threaten him with his cat, or did he just tell him what was going to happen, and he did it? And why is he suddenly giving me the building project? Because you fucked me in the front seat of his car or is it because of me being there when his kid decided to make an appearance? Either way, I'm not taking it." Neal pulled into a large drive and waved to the man at the gate as it opened. "This is not going to work out."

He stopped the car and turned in the seat to look at her. "Okay first question, yes, I did know that he'd gotten the money owed to you by Sanders, and I told him after the fact when I found out that you'd be pissed. He said that he wanted to help you, and he'd done it before I knew it. And he wants me to be your accountant. Secondly, if you're going to blame everything on you and I having sex on the front seat of this car, I'm going to bend you over my knee and beat that luscious ass of yours until I come all over you. He was already going to give you the project before any of this. The others hadn't worked out the way he'd wanted them to, and after looking over your drawings, he could see what you'd come up with, and they both decided to give it to the person who had what Ryland and Bronwyn wanted in mind, not what the florist wanted."

Her mind had stuttered to a stop when he said he was going to beat her butt. She looked at him, realizing what else he'd said. "How did he get my drawings?"

"I don't know. Your mom, maybe?" He looked out the window and then back at her. "This is my home, and I'd very much like for you to come inside and meet Carl while I get some things gathered up. I shouldn't be more than twenty minutes."

"I'm sorry." He nodded and got out. She had hurt him, but it didn't keep him from coming around to her side of the car and opening the door for her. She looked up at him. "I am sorry."

"It's fine, Rayne, I promise. But you need to trust me, and when you fly off the handle like that, I have to work hard not to pull you over my knee and...." He took a deep breath. "It's me. I should have told you when Ryland told me what he'd done. I think he spoke to the others as well. You might be happy to know that he's a good man and his heart is in the right place, but he's a pain in my ass too."

They went into the house by way of the kitchen. She was overwhelmed when they entered the biggest room she'd been in besides her showroom. She was just looking at the double-wide refrigerator after Neal had left her there when a man stepped out of what she thought was a pantry.

"Well, hello there, miss." He was as wide as he was tall, but he didn't frighten her like a lot of big men did. "I'm Carl Winchester, cook and chief of this place. You're the new mate."

She flushed, knowing just how he'd figured that out. Neal's scent would be all over her right now. She wanted to take a long shower but was pretty sure from what her mom had told her a long time ago that the scent of a mate would never wear off.

"Rayne Morrow, and yes, I guess I am. Neal went to gather some things to wear at work in the morning. He said he's going to work for me, but I don't really need him because my mom said she'd be there, but there is no telling him that because he...." She took a deep breath, and he smiled at her. "I'm nervous."

"I can see that too. Are you hungry? I was just about to toss together some dinner for me and the rest of the staff. We thought that Mr. Neal was going to his mother's for supper."

"He was, but Bronwyn had her baby, and they all went to the hospital." He nodded as he put something on the counter. He started pulling things from the refrigerator she'd been admiring.

"I'd heard she'd had the baby. She's a lovely woman." He handed her a knife and a head of lettuce. She sat them both down. "You don't wish to help?"

"I know nothing about cooking. My mom does but not me. I can barely open a can of soup without nearly cutting my fingers off." She took a step back as he laughed. "I'm not kidding. I will hurt something if I try."

He handed her the lettuce. "Then tear it up. No bigger than an inch and a half. I'll do the rest of the cutting. Then when Margaret comes in, we'll put her to work with you. Shouldn't be any more than a minute or two."

A woman of about fifty came into the room and smiled at her. Carl introduced her to the woman, and she took over the lettuce and gave her a peeler to do the carrots. In no time, she had several large carrots ready and was peeling two cucumbers when Neal walked in. She set everything down only to have Neal hand them back to her and stand behind her as she cut up the carrots and other vegetables. He laughed with Carl when he told him about her inability to cook.

"You'll stay to eat then?" Neal looked at her when Carl asked. She was having fun, and the smells coming from the pots on the stove made her mouth water. She nodded and told him if he didn't mind, she didn't either. Forty minutes later, she and Neal were sitting at the large kitchen table with all of his staff, all eight of them having the best spaghetti and marinara sauce she'd ever eaten.

"We try and have a meal together at least once a week, but lately, I've been a little too busy to enjoy this." Neal asked her if she wanted more pasta, and she shook her head as he continued. "Carl has been working for me since I bought this house. Actually, he came with the house when I bought it, as did his wife, Margaret. Then over the ensuing years, the rest of his family joined us."

Neal grinned around the table, and she looked at them all as he introduced them all to her. They were very nice, all of them were. When Carl started to clear the plates, she stood up and gathered a few as well. He told her to have a seat and that he'd made dessert for them. She was surprised when he pulled a smallish cake from the deepness of the refrigerator and presented it to her and Neal. It had so many flowers on it that she knew that he'd done this for them.

"We'd heard, you see, that he'd taken a mate. We were to have a dinner for you tomorrow night when he brought you by, but you turned up tonight. Bronwyn warned us you might be coming, and I hurried through this one." He handed her a knife. "Don't cut anything but the cake, mistress, and welcome to the Golden family."

She was so touched by what they'd done that she had to swallow several times before she could speak. They had done this because she was Neal's mate. Looking around the room at them, she wondered how they would treat her if they knew what she was and tried her best to shrug it off. Neal kissed her wrist as she held the knife and took it from her. He was serving the others their cake when she found her tongue.

"Thank you all so much. I…I don't know what to say. This was the kindest thing you could have done for me." Carl nodded as he took a healthy bite of his cake. She opened her mouth when Neal told her to and moaned when he put a piece of the cake in her mouth. She could get used to this kind of treatment.

Chapter 7

They were pulling onto her street when they noticed the line of cars the next morning. Neal was almost afraid to ask her if this was her usual Saturday morning rush when his cell phone rang. He handed it to her, and she answered it.

"It's your brother, Ryland. He needs to speak to you." He took the phone from her as he navigated through the traffic to where she was telling him to go at the back of the shop near her apartment. He'd never seen so many cars.

"Are you on your way to work?" He told him he was going to the shop with Rayne. "That's what I mean. I'm here now. I thought you said you guys would be in at six."

"We got sidetracked." He looked over at Rayne and smiled when she blushed. "I think you've been sidetracked a few times yourself since you took a mate." He wouldn't tell his brother that having sex in bed was by far better than he'd ever had before. As well as the tub, the office, and also his closet for that matter. Hell, any place was a good place to have sex as far as he was concerned. He couldn't wait to try out the other rooms in the house.

"Well, I'm here along with the rest of the family. Bronwyn is home, of course, but we...can you please get your asses here before there's a riot?" He heard Rayne say his name, and he turned to look where she was pointing. The cars were lined up in front of her little shop, and there were at least fifty people standing in line to get in. He asked his brother what he'd done.

"I just told a few people. I swear. I did take out the ad in the paper, but it wasn't a whole page. Bronwyn said that would be for later. Then there were the calls mom made. Not that many, just to her garden club and her quilting club." Neal relayed the information to Rayne, who nodded.

"How am I going to help this many people today? I have two trucks coming in this morning and another this afternoon after I close. If I can close. What am I going to do?" He was suddenly panicky because she was.

He said everything to his brother, trying really hard not to upset the woman who was currently gripping the handle so tightly he was sure she was going to break it off. He could run the register a little but not like her, or her mom did. He almost missed what his brother was saying.

"What do you mean one is there now? At the shop?" Ryland said he and Brock were unloading the truck but were running out of room to put things in her showroom. Could they please hurry? Neal pulled up behind the building and saw them all standing there with Ryland on his cell. As soon as he hung up, he made his way to them.

"I had to break in to help out. You need a better security system." He grinned. "We didn't know where you wanted things. I'm thinking you should just have the sale out here, but I think that you might run out of room here too." Rayne glared at him and walked to the driver, who was still helping them pull things off. "I think she's pissed at me. Is it because I broke in or because of the lines of people coming in?"

Neal glared at his brother. "You think? What the fuck were you thinking? She's terrified. She's not used to this sort of help, and, frankly, I'm a little terrified myself. I said I'd help her."

"We all are. I already sent Jules in, and he's working with her mom to get the register down pat. Mom and Ally are walking around the floor so they can find things. Those maps she had on the counter helped out a lot."

Neal walked away from his brother. It was that or kill him. Rayne was just loading up a stack of ceramic pots to take inside when he found her. She looked ready to cry. He took her into his arms.

"I'm going to be swamped, and all I can think about is how badly I want to kill Ryland. Or maybe hug him. This is going to help me pay off my mom sooner if I can manage to sell anything today." He told her she would do fine and his family was going to help them. "I need to get this in and open up. I guess two hours early isn't going to hurt me."

The floor flooded with people as soon as she unlocked the doors. He had suggested that they open a second register, and she told him she didn't have one. Ryland sent someone to get one against her wishes, but he had a feeling they were going to need it. Rayne was finishing putting the first truck on the floor as the second one, this one with flowers and soil, pulled in. Christ, he didn't realize how much inventory you could get on one of those suckers. And not only that but the amount of inventory she needed to run just a flower shop like this one.

By nine-thirty, she was up to her elbows putting together planters that were selling as fast as she got them completed. He was helping as best he could, but sometimes she'd move faster than him, and he'd miss a flower or two. But it didn't seem to matter. If it wasn't nailed down and had a price tag on it, people were buying it. By eleven, there didn't seem to be an end in sight, and that's when Carl and the rest of his staff showed up with lunch.

Sandwiches were passed out among the family, and everyone ate while they worked. He was sure that he'd eaten dirt a couple of times, but he didn't care. He loved what was going on now that he had a chance to see that it was working. When the next truck pulled in, he went out to unload the trees and another round of flowers and soil. He asked the man where he was taking the rest of the merchandise he had on the truck. He said it was a back haul. He told him that the last stop didn't want it, and he had to take it back to where he'd picked all this up at. After a few calls, Neal was able to get the company to sell him all that was on the truck for twenty-five cents on the dollar. The driver was so thrilled he didn't have to drive it back that he helped unload it and even hung around to help load a few cars with their purchases. Said he didn't want to fight that traffic again if he didn't have to.

Things started to slow around two, and by four, they were finishing up with the last customer. Rayne had been working nonstop on several planters that were going to be picked up in an hour, and he went back to help her. Her mom was sitting there talking to her with his mom.

"I don't care, sweetheart, but we should really consider it. Even if my calculations are even half right, you've done more business today than you did all of last year. You can afford to hire some extra help." His mom nodded as she picked up the thread.

"And think of the business you'll have once the front lobby is finished. My goodness, there will be people lined up at the door." Rayne looked at her. "Okay, that was a bad reference, but I, for one, had a blast today. Who knew that so many flowers could be put together in one little vase and look so lovely?"

"I did. And I can't expand yet. I still owe more on this place than I can afford during the off months, and in a few months, no one will want planters. They'll want to see fall things...then Christmas. I don't know how to do that."

"I can." They all three looked at him. "I know a great deal about marketing, and there is no reason you have to close for any more than a month, like in January. I think with the right merchandising, you could do a great business year-round. Especially if you wanted to bring in live Christmas trees, as well as cut ones."

She looked up at him. "You have your own business to work at. And this is...today was a fluke, people coming in out of a sense of duty because your brother told them to." He shook his head. "Are you telling me that most of these people here don't have some sort of connection to the Golden family?"

"Most of them did, yes. I won't argue with that, but no one asked them to spend as much as they did. And I'm sure that's what they came here to do when they pulled up too. Fulfill a request from a very powerful and rich family and nothing more. But no one told them to spend hundreds of dollars like they did. Mrs. Patterson, a friend of my mom's, spent nearly a thousand dollars and gushed about it the entire time. Mr. Gable told me he'd never seen this place before the ad came out in the paper and only came out to shake your hand and to buy a posy or two for the missus. He left here with over five hundred dollars worth of posies as well as the order you're doing now for his law office." Their moms left, and he sat down in front of her. "And I made a deal with your distributor when the last truck came in. He said that he'd sell you all the backload merchandise you could handle for a quarter of the price he was selling it for just so he won't have to haul it back. Not to mention he said he'd give you a thirty percent discount if you were to pay net thirty."

"I don't have that sort of money, Neal. Do you have any idea how much all this cost me already? If it wasn't for net ninety, I couldn't make this work at all right now." He took her hand as she continued. "I only wanted to do this to be able to live. Those sorts of terms, net thirty and buying merchandise that I can't afford, will make it so I can't."

"I was going to talk to you about this later, but now seems to be a great time. You need a partner, one with money to spend and a great deal of personal interest in your business." She looked at him. "As much as I would like to say it's me, I can't do that. We're going to be a couple, and I don't want money to be an issue with us over a business deal. I was talking about Golden Enterprises. I would be a part of it, but not as close as I would normally."

"I don't want a partner." She moved her hand through the dirt, and he watched the plants she'd put in it seem to grow as he watched them. "I would love to make this business bigger than it is, but taking on a partner like your brother would make me have to do things I don't want to do."

"Like what, love? You can pretty much write your own ticket here as you're going to be the one doing most of the work while all he does is rake in the profits with you." She snorted, and he leaned back in the chair and pulled the last two pots toward them as she moved the one she'd been working on out of the way.

"I can't do this from a prison cell, and I'm sure that's where I'd be if he were to try and boss me around." Neal lowered his head and tried hard to hide the smile. "Not to mention your sister-in-law is bossy. I don't need another mother."

"Good thing, too, since I don't want to be your flipping mother. And you should also know that as your partner, I'd expect a big discount too." Bronwyn moved into the room and sat down. "Hello, Rayne. I heard you had a good day. Wanna do it again Monday?"

~~~

It was nearly seven o'clock before they all moved out to their cars. They were going to the diner to eat, and her mom was nervous and excited to have them there. Rayne was so tired that she just wanted to sit down and eat anything that was put in front of her.

She'd placed another order, too, while Neal and his brothers cleaned up. Her mom and Mrs. Golden watered what little was left in the showroom as well as the trees. Ally helped her count out the deposit as well as double-checked that all the orders had been fulfilled, and gave her a list of what needed to be done and where it had to go. Ally was very organized.

"I could do this. I could help you get your orders in line and do the paperwork for you. I'm driving our cook insane being at home all the time. I worked for Alistair for a little while, but that didn't work for us." Rayne asked if they fought a lot, and Ally grinned. "No, we were constantly having sex on the desk, in the break room, anywhere we could. We weren't getting a damned thing done working together."

Rayne blushed. She thought about this morning and how hard it had been to get out of the house. Every time he touched her, she wanted to throw Neal down and have her way with him. Ally laughed as if she could read her mind.

"Wait until he changes you. Christ, sex as a tiger is amazingly wonderful." Her skin tightened over her body, and she looked up to see Neal coming toward them. Ally laughed and left the room, telling her that she would love to come in and work for her starting Monday.

He sat down next to her in the restaurant just as their dinner was being served. She looked down at her plate and wondered what she'd ordered when he kissed her neck. She looked up at him, dazed.

"I think we can assume that you're more tired than you've ever been, but you need to eat." She had nodded at him while he picked up her fork and handed it to her. "Ryland had a locksmith come by and fix the door he'd broken. He said that you can make him feel better by putting in a better security system."

"I don't have a security system at all, and I think he knows that." He laughed. "Did you tell him I don't need a sitter? That I know what I'm doing?"

"I think he figured that out today. You impressed him and the rest of my family by what you managed to accomplish today. He said he'd have you work for him if he wasn't afraid of you murdering him in his office one day." He took her fork and cut off a piece of…it smelled like curry chicken…and put it in her mouth. It was definitely curried chicken, and she moaned as the taste exploded in her mouth.

His own fork stilled halfway to his mouth, and he turned to her slowly. "Do you have any idea how many times I've wanted to find you and take you to the floor until you screamed my name?"

"No. I thought you were too busy for that." He shook his head and slid his hand along her thigh. "Stop that. Your family is right here."

He leaned in and nipped at her ear lobe, and she felt as if he'd set her on fire. "I know where they are and where I'd like for us to be as well. I want to take you home and do all the things I didn't get to do to you last night or this morning."

He'd done a great many things to her last night, some of which had required some of his ties and a large feather he'd taken from the duster. She'd never been tied up before and had never come so hard in her life when he'd used the feather over her clit and nipples. When she shivered, he grinned at her and told her to eat.

"I would like to speak to you. Now, if you wouldn't mind."

She looked up at Ryland when he sat down next to her. Her entire body was on fire, and he wanted to speak to her? Not if he wanted it to be something that was coherent.

Neal moved away and sat near his mom. She figured that whatever Ryland had to say to her was private, and she wondered if this was where he forbade her to see Neal again. She didn't know why that hurt so much, but it did. So before he could tell her that she had to back off, she decided she'd do it for him.

"I didn't want this in the first place. I told him to stay away, but like all men, you figure you know what's best for us poor helpless females. Well, I don't care what you say about us not being together, so you can just fuck the hell off." He looked at her oddly, then threw back his head and laughed. She was so confused that she stood up to leave him to his unexpected mirth.

"Sit down, Rayne, and let me tell you the real reason I'm here. And by the way, have you met my wife? Does she strike you as someone who would let me even for a minute treat her like she was poor or helpless?" She sat down, and he nodded. "That was a really good one. What did you plan to do? Storm out and have me face the wrath of everyone in this room alone?"

She shook her head. "I thought you were here to tell me to stay away from your family and that, I don't know, I wasn't good enough for Neal. I don't understand you people."

"Good, because, honey, we don't understand you either. But as for you not being good enough for Neal? That's not even close to the truth. You're everything he needs and then some." He laughed again. "You didn't really think I came here to tell you to fuck off, did you?"

"Yes." He laughed again. "I really don't get you. You have all the money in the world, and yet you all came in and helped me today when...granted, most of it was your fault anyway, but you could have let me fail. I thought about it a lot today, and I don't understand why you did it. For me."

"You're family now, and we help each other. And it wasn't just for you but for Neal as well. He would have felt as if he failed you had today not worked out, even though I'd made the decision to help you." He leaned back in his chair and handed her a thick file. "That's the contract for the lobby of our main building downtown. There are six other buildings that we'd like for you to maintain too, and there are contracts in there for those as well. I understand from your mom that you do that. Go back to make sure the plants are up to your standards and replace or fix what needs it."

"Yes, but I don't have the resources to take on a job this big. I have some capital now that Sanders is going to pay me, but not on this scale." She started to hand him back the file when an envelope fell out. "What's this?"

"It's a deposit. I'm hoping it's substantial enough to give you the extra capital to do the job for us." She opened the envelope and looked up at him. "Is it?"

"You know it is. It's more than you know I was going to charge you to do the initial project." She put the check back in the envelope and stuffed it in the file, and laid it on the table beside them. "Why are you doing this? If this has anything to do with your daughter, I don't want the job this way. I have standards. They aren't as high or as lofty as the Goldens', but they're all I have."

He stared at her for several minutes, but she didn't squirm. She wanted to and felt the need to fidget like she'd never felt before. When he picked up the file and handed her the first contract, she looked at where he was pointing.

"As you can see, this was drawn up the day before my daughter was delivered safely by you. And the other six the morning you delivered her and gave my wife a chance to survive when all I wanted to do was panic. And as for wanting you to do this because of a sense of obligation because of all this, then no, I wouldn't stay in business very long if I let my emotions lead me by the short hairs, as my father used to say." She took the pen he offered her. "I'm not willing to have a second-rate company being the first thing people see when they come into my lobby. And I doubt for one second that you'd give me that. Sign the fucking contracts, Rayne, and I'll get down to the other part of my business with you."

She scribbled her name over all the places that he'd had marked with tabs. She supposed she should have read it over or at least had an attorney do it. But the only one she knew was more than likely the one who had written this one, and she couldn't afford anything else. Besides, as much as she hated to admit it even to herself, she trusted the male cat in front of her.

"Now, I would like to become a silent partner to your company. And this has nothing to do with the previous contract signed by us both. We can make a great deal of money off this venture, and I, for one, like money. Do you?" She nodded at him before she could think. "Good. Here is what I propose for us as a beginning."

By the time she'd left the restaurant, she was a great deal smarter about what the Golden Towers did, and she would have a nice bank account when she was able to get to hers in the morning. She looked down at the checks Ryland had given her, as well as a copy of the contracts that Alistair just happened to have on him. When Ryland, then her mom, signed off as investor and witness, she sat back and then stood up.

"I need air. Now. I need some air." She left the little dining area and was out the door before anyone could stop her. She was taking big gulps of night air when she felt Neal come out behind her.

"Did he hurt you?" She turned to laugh when she realized that he was serious. "Ryland can be a bit pushy when he wants something. But he'd asked me to give the two of you a few minutes. So I ask again, did he hurt you?"

"No. He bought a small interest in my business, hired me as an outside consultant to help with the books, and gave me a list of places I could get cheap labor during the peak times. He also gave me over seven hundred thousand dollars in the form of cashier's checks for his first installment of buying a percentage of my... Christ, who has that kind of money?"

"We do." He helped her to the bench when she swayed. "Don't move while I get you something to drink."

When he returned, she looked up at him. "You knew he was going to do this. Why didn't you tell me?"

"Because you needed to hear it from him, as I have very little to do with it, and as far as now, we're mates, but it's still your business. Drink this. It's water." She took a sip and handed him the file that Alistair gave her. "Is this the contract?"

"Contracts, as in plural. He wants me to do the other buildings that you guys own too. Also, he wants me to think about expanding my business to run year-round." She sat back and eyed him. "I wonder where he might have gotten that idea."

He flushed but didn't say anything as he sat beside her. "So you're a wealthy woman now. What do you want to do to celebrate?"

A thousand and one things popped into her head, and not one of them could they do there. She stood up and leaned down to bite his ear. He wrapped his hand into her hair and held her to him as she licked the curve in his ear, then down along his throat to his pounding pulse. When he stood up, he nearly dragged her to the car. Instead of going to the front like she'd thought he would, he opened the back end and started to strip down.

"I'm going to shift. Then I'm going to find you and then fuck you." He tore his shirt off and tossed it in the back of the car. "I would suggest that you take off those shoes and run. Because I'm not going to wait too much longer before I'm naked and running after you."

Throwing everything she had in her hands on top of his things, she kicked off her shoes and took off as fast as she could for the tree line. Even as her heart felt as if it were pounding out of her chest, she felt her body's need of this man as it rolled through her veins like molten lava.

Chapter 8

Sheldon Pierce had one more name on his list, and if this one didn't pan out, he was going to have to go back to his old job, knowing that everyone was right. There were no such things as weretigers. He stopped at the large front gate and pushed the buzzer. When the large man came out of his booth that Sheldon had not seen until that moment, he thought maybe he'd just go home anyway.

"I'm looking for Bronwyn Lawrence Golden. I was told she lived here now." The man didn't say anything, but for reasons Sheldon couldn't explain, he felt the need to give the man more than he needed to. "I'm investigating the disappearance of a man by the name of Cunningham, Eli Cunningham. Do you know of him?"

"You see that road behind you?" Sheldon turned and looked at it, thinking the man was going to give him directions to finding the woman. "You turn your vehicle around and pull out onto it. Hopefully, there might be a big fucking truck coming, but I got a feeling that I'm not going to be so lucky. But you pull out anyway, and then you turn and never look back this way again. Because you know what happens if you do?"

Sheldon shook his head. He was afraid of the answer and also what the bear of a man would do to him as well. When he leaned down to put his face less than an inch from his, Sheldon whimpered.

"What happens is I pull you from your car through the window whether it's open or not and beat the living shit out of you, then toss you into the pit I have behind my station there and let you rot with the other motherfucking pricks that come here looking for a handout."

He started to tell the man he wasn't there for a handout when he hit the roof of Sheldon's car, and it bent toward his head. He put his car in reverse so fast that he knew that the gears were grinding. Had there been a truck coming in either direction, he would have been dead because he never looked when he pulled out of the drive and right into the street. He was nearly a mile away before his heart began to slow.

His phone was ringing, and he had to pull over to answer it. He was shaking so hard that he nearly hung up on the call twice before he got his finger to slide the tab over for him to speak into it. He nearly wet himself when the person on the other end said her name.

"Bronwyn Lawrence is your girl." Sheldon asked his nephew and jack-of-all-trades helper, Bobby Smyth, what he meant. "About ten years ago or so, she was in that same lab, and I found pictures of her. She's a beauty too. And just over a year ago, she and some rich prick married, and she is now Bronwyn Golden. Same girl."

"Those pictures were shit, Bobby, like I told you before I left. You can't even tell if she's a girl, much less what she looks like." He felt the weight of the roof of his car press down on him, and he tried to shove it back into place. How the hell that man had done that was beyond him. "Just...I'm coming home. This is a dead end."

"I have this amazing little program that can take pictures like the ones in her file and enhance them, make them more…readable. It's her. I'm sending you a copy of what I found and what I was able to get from my work here. You call me back when you get them."

Sheldon didn't hold out any hope and drove to the closest restaurant he could find to have dinner and to view the email. He heard it alert him that he'd received some but didn't pull over this time to see it. Bobby had been sending him shit all month.

After ordering the nightly special of meatloaf and mashed potatoes, he waited until his coleslaw and tea were brought before he went through the process of pulling his email up. He was just having his empty salad plate taken away when the thing finally loaded. One of these days, he was going to get a better phone but hadn't found a reason to yet. It might be time to replace it now. When the first picture popped up, he knew this was the one from the paper. He had a copy of it in the file back at this hotel along with the other nineteen Bronwyns he'd had on his list. When the second photo was being loaded, the waitress sat his dinner plate in front of him, and he could only stare at it.

"Something wrong there, sweetie?" He looked up at her and then at the plate. "You did order the special, didn't you?"

"Yes. But this is…I've never had…is this one portion?" She laughed and told him she'd be back. On his plate was the biggest hunk of meatloaf he'd ever seen as well as about two cups of mashed potatoes. And the green beans were just like his mom used to make, onions and tiny little potatoes as well as what looked like ham. He was in heaven. When she put a basket of cornbread in front of him, he actually considered asking her to marry him. He put the first bite into his mouth and moaned. Christ, he was going to ask her as soon as she came back.

Sheldon finished his entire meal and had four glasses of the sweetest tea he'd ever drunk along with it. Christ, he was so full he felt like he was going to pop a button. He was reading the menu to see what to have for dessert when his phone rang. He nearly didn't answer it, not wanting his nephew to intrude on his fine dining when he noticed people staring. He answered it on the fourth ring.

"Well? It's her, isn't it?" He had to think about what he was talking about when he remembered the picture. "I knew it."

"I been having dinner, and I've not looked at it if you want to know the truth. Let me call you back in ten minutes." He asked for his check after hanging up on Bobby and was in his car again when he pulled up the pictures. He nearly went back inside to ask the waitress if what he was seeing was true. It was Bronwyn right down to the pissed-off look in her eyes.

He called Bobby back and tried to tone down his excitement. "Give me her address, and I'll check it out in person in the morning. If it's her, I'll—"

"It's her. You and I both know it. And you said I could come to you when you found this woman. And you'd tell me what she is to the CIA. I helped you, and now you have to help me." He had been under the impression that Bobby would have had to have been a great deal more help and a lot less annoying when he'd agreed to those terms. He told him he would see her tomorrow, and after that, he'd call him.

After going back to his hotel room and pulling up the email on his laptop, he could see that Bobby had been right. There was no question that this woman and the one from the older pictures were the same women. He moved to his bed, thinking about what he was going to say to her. He wanted her to come back with him so he could prove to everyone that he wasn't nuts, but he wasn't stupid enough to think that would ever work either. She was as good as his.

He pulled out the address he'd gone to yesterday. The directions that he'd found had led him to a lab that was so far off the beaten path that he would never have found it without the navigation device on his phone. He had knocked on the front door only to find it unmanned and unlocked. He had walked in and had been surprised by what he'd seen.

There were so many men and women walking around with white coats and small laptops that he wondered where the funding was coming from. It struck him as some covert operation, and it was confirmed by one of the security officers that asked him who he had been there to see.

The man was wearing a government-issued Glock as well as a badge that said CIA. He showed him his identification, and the man nodded and told him to wait while he gave him an official badge for the facility.

"This way, no one will question you again, Mr. Pierce." With his newly printed badge, he had walked around for hours just taking it all in. He'd even been able to walk in some of the more restricted areas. And that's when he figured out where he could take Bronwyn when he had her. And now, he just about had her where he wanted her. And he would have her soon too.

~~~

"Hi." Rayne nodded to the man sitting at her desk in the shop. "Ryland asked me to come over and have a look at your books."

She took her raincoat to the little lunchroom and pulled out her phone. Just before the call was connected, the man came into the room behind her, and she felt the bite of the gun in her back. He told her to come with him.

"No, I don't think so." He pressed the gun in harder, and she let herself fall forward. As soon as he reached for her, she assumed to keep her from falling, she used his off-balanced weight and flipped him over her shoulder and onto his back. Before he could get up, she wrapped her hand around his head and held him.

The voice on the phone alerted her that she might have dialed someone, and she groaned when she realized it was Bronwyn rather than Neal like she'd meant to call. She told the woman what had happened.

"I'm sending Brock to deal with him. Is he secure?" Rayne didn't have a clue what she meant and asked her. "I mean, my dear, are you holding him with some of that awesomely wicked power of yours or do you have him tied to a chair?"

"Holding him. Which would you find more secure, just out of curiosity?" Bronwyn laughed and told her that she thought the way she had him was better. "I hope so because I can't see if anyone else is in here with him."

"Good point. I think you should contact Neal too. He's probably felt your fear by now and will no doubt be trying to contact you. Have you been using your link to speak to him?"

He'd shown her how to use it last night when he'd nearly killed her with a climax. When she disconnected the call with Bronwyn, she'd told Neal she was fine, but there had been an intruder in her office. He told her he was on his way. She sat down on the floor, still holding the man as she waited for someone to show up.

It was a good twenty-five minutes later when Neal showed. Brock was only ten minutes behind him. She'd been surprised to see both Keith and Jules show up, but they had come by on an unrelated quest. Keith wanted to set up her computer, and Jules wanted to ask her if he could display his pottery in her shop.

"I won't bring in any of my larger pieces unless you want them." He'd grinned at her as she held the man down until Brock took him and the gun. "I just think it might bring in some of the… the clientele that buys my stuff."

"Snobs, you mean." He laughed. "I guess if you want. But you have to make sure that you have some sort of barrier put around it. I don't have the insurance to cover that kind of work if some kid decided to break it."

He told her he had a rider on his insurance he carried that covered it. She was just showing him how much space he could have when Brock and Neal walked toward her. Christ, it was only Monday, and she was having a shitty week already.

"He was alone, and you're never going to guess who sent him." She already knew and told Brock. He looked so crestfallen that she had to laugh. "I did get to talk to him before you arrived. And I can make him tell me the truth. How did you get it out of him?"

"I beat the shit out of him." She laughed until she realized he was serious. "I guess your way was better, but mine was way more fun. And a great way to relieve some of that pent-up stress I've been having."

The police were called in, and she told them what the would-be kidnapper had told her. "He works for Daniel Sanders, and the man owes me a great deal of money that is well past due. I pressed charges against him the other day, and this is how he repays me. He sent that man here to tell me to back off and that he wasn't paying me what he owed me any more than he was giving me back my things. I'd like to press charges against both men if that's possible."

The officer taking her statement, looked at her. "Are you sure, ma'am? He's sort of got a lot of money, and he can be a little on the…I've only heard that he has a temper, but I'd hate to have him take it out on a pretty girl like you."

She had to cough loudly to cover the growl that came from Neal. He seemed to grow bigger the more she looked at him, and she was pretty sure that the officer had seen it as well. Neal's cat was beautiful, but she was pretty sure if he came out now, it wouldn't be for fun like it had been yesterday and the day before. She decided to deal with the cop on her own before Neal ate him for a snack.

"Mr. Sanders owes me nearly twelve thousand dollars, officer. Does the fact that he has more money than me make it okay for him to send in men with guns to have me forget about it? Do you have twelve grand that you can just toss away?" He shook his head. "Neither do I. I want to press charges against him. Either you take my statement, or I'll have my lawyer come down there and talk to your captain."

The officer took her statement and told her that he'd make sure the proper paperwork was filed. After he left, it took her another hour to get everyone out, and then Ally showed up. She smiled and told her to do her thing, and she'd do what she did best. As long as she didn't bother her, she said to go for it.

Arranging the orders was a simple task. She mingled the larger orders in with the smaller ones, so she had something to keep her energy levels about the same all day. She had learned that doing the larger orders first left her with little energy to do the smaller ones, and doing the little ones first sort of bored her. She put everything on her carts, still nervous about all the inventory that she had in the storeroom and on the floor. She set to work.

She didn't play music when she worked, and when the speaker came to life, playing some classical music in her little room, she noticed that it was just nine o'clock. Her mom, she figured, had opened the store up and knew if she needed her, she knew where to find her. Smiling, she thought of being found by Neal the other night.

Christ, when she'd taken off for the woods, she'd been excited. Not afraid, though now that she had time to think about it, she probably should have been. But he'd made it sound fun and erotic. When she hid behind the first tree and tried to calm her breaths, he'd walked right by her and rubbed his furred body against her. She'd nearly screamed when he turned to look at her and growled.

"You're making this too easy." His voice echoed in her mind, and she felt his need. *"I want you to hide from me. Run if you have to but make me chase you. And the next time I can find you, you'll take off a piece of your clothing."*

"I can't do that. What if someone sees me?" He told her that he'd know if someone came within a mile of her. "And what do I get in return if you never find me?"

He moved toward her and licked her arm from wrist to elbow. Her entire body felt it all the way from the tip of her toes, which curled under to the top of her head. Even her pussy felt him. His sharp command to run had her taking off again and this time running hard.

He'd found her twice more. Once she'd been hiding in a dead log, and he'd licked her bare foot. When she'd crawled out, dirty and feeling like she wanted to quit, he told her to take off her shirt. Tossing it to the ground, he'd licked her belly, and she moaned. Without being told, she took off again.

She wasn't sure if she was getting better at hiding or if he was teasing her. She figured it had taken him at least double the time to find her that time. But when he'd told her to take off her pants, she nearly told him no. Then she watched him stare at her as she backed against the tree she'd been hiding in.

He was hungry and not for anything from the restaurant this time. He wanted her, and the longer he stared at her, the more she wanted him to take her. Moving slowly, she unsnapped her pants and pulled them off, leaving her panties where they were. This time when he came toward her, all she could think about was his wet, rough tongue.

She cried out as he buried his nose against her wet thighs. "Neal, I don't want to play anymore. I need you."

"Take them off. I want to drink from you." She shook her head, not caring how he drank from her but wanting him to strip her. *"Rayne, my cat will have his taste whether you give it freely or not."*

"No. You want me. You have to take me." She watched as he licked her knee. Then he moved closer to her. His tongue licked a path to her hip, and he took the small bit of lace into his mouth and, with a growl, tore them from her. She was breathing so hard she was sure he could hear her. Then he shifted to himself, his human self.

Opening her legs for him, she felt him taste her. Even as he lapped at her, devoured her, she wanted more. She whimpered when he stood up as she begged him to take her. His hands were soon at her shoulders and holding her against the tree. This time the shift was different like he'd been holding back before.

Neal was taller than her as a human, and his cat was bigger as well. He was so close to her that she could see how sharp his teeth were, how long and vicious they were. When he licked her shoulder, she moaned again, and when he sank his teeth into her, she screamed loudly.

"I love you," he said to her even as he lifted his head. *"I love you so very much."*

He dropped to his feet and put his paws on her hips. She watched him, still dizzy from his bite, as his paws changed; fingers grew from the ends as his hand emerged. His skin seemed to absorb his cat, fur smoothed out, and his muscles seemed to emerge stronger, thicker.

He never stopped looking at her as his body went from beast to man. Though he'd been no less beast than he'd been before, he was hers. Looking into his eyes, she could see the color there. His cat still stared back at her.

Biting her gently, she moaned each time. He bit her on her hip, then her thigh, her waist. Then he moved up her body to her breasts and nipples. Her fingers were suckled into his mouth only to be bitten as well. Each time he drew blood, and every time he licked the tiny wound closed.

"Do you know what I'm doing to you?" She started to nod and tell him he was marking her, but she was sure that wasn't it. "I'm changing you."

Her heart leapt in her throat. "Why?" When he bit into her calf, she felt him tear into muscle, but as soon as the pain registered, it was gone.

"Because the next time we do this, I'm going to run after my mate and not your human." He nipped at her wrist and let the blood fall from the wound into his mouth before sealing the wound. "Because my cat is hungry for yours, he wants to bend you down over the ground and take you hard and fast. Fill you with his cum and bite you hard enough to have you scream through it."

"What if I didn't want this?" He grinned up at her. "I'm serious. What if I didn't want to be your cat?"

His hands ran up her thighs, and he slid his finger into her sheath. She rode his finger as he pressed a second, then a third into her. When he suckled her clit into his mouth, she came, screaming his name, and he lifted his head. She was so close again that she begged him to take her.

"Do you know how much I hold back when I fuck you? How

gentle I have to be not to hurt you when we make love?" She shook her head. "When my cat takes yours, he won't be gentle. He won't care if you come or not. He'll only want to run you down, fuck you from behind and bite you. I want to plow into you as well, Rayne. I want to take you hard and watch you as my cock almost hurts you I'm so deep. I want to bite you while my cock fills you, and when I roll you to your belly and ram my cock deep into your ass, you'll come then, too, screaming at me more than you've ever imagined. And you'll be able to take me."

She was so ready and wet her body hurt. Even as she pulled his head to her pussy, she felt his tongue enter her. Riding him, she begged him to fuck her. Begged him to finish her. When she was suddenly on her back, he entered her. His cock felt as if he were at her womb, and she knew that he was going to hurt her.

"Come. Come now, and I'll fill you." His command had her soaring over the top, but before she could land, he was bringing her again and again. When he lifted her ass, tilted it upward, he went deeper still, and she cried out.

"Say it, Rayne. Tell me you want this, and I'll finish you." She could barely breathe around the pounding of her heart. And when he slammed deeper still, she screamed out her consent and felt his teeth take her throat.

"Rayne?" She looked up from the planter she was holding and tried to wrap her mind around the person standing in front of her. She said her name twice more before she could see that it was Ally, and she was smiling at her.

"I was...I was thinking about something." When Ally laughed, she flushed. "Is it always like this with them?"

"Yes." She handed her a sandwich. "I came in here around lunchtime, but you grunted at me, so I left you alone. I can see now that when you get in a zone, you really go there."

Rayne looked around the room. She'd been busy. But she didn't see all that much that would make her think she'd been in a zone. When one of the helpers that Ally had introduced her to this morning came in, he had a cart filled with flowers and rolled it next to the one filled with dirt. She looked at Ally when she laughed.

"Come with me." She walked from her work area to just outside and nearly fell back. "This is the fifth time he's brought you stuff. The last time he brought you double what you have now, so I'm figuring by the time I let you go back to wherever you were, he'll have brought you more than that. You've been very busy."

There were crocks and planters everywhere. Not just on the shelves and tables but under them and around them. She walked around and saw that she'd done hanging baskets as well. Flowers and vines overflowed them until they hung a foot from their pots. Large blossoms of pansies dripped from bowls, and cactus sat in small containers with small rocks and paper flowers. She watched as a fig tree moved by her on someone's cart with jade planted at its base and small feathered birds in its branches. She looked at Ally as she stood beside her.

"I won't be able to sell all this." Ally laughed. "I mean it. I don't know what I was thinking, but…that's not true. I know just what I was thinking, but this, this is too much."

"You've sold nearly a quarter of what you've completed. And there are orders for some of the customers that have left and will return by the weekend. I started taking pictures of them in the event you wanted to put things online. You're not going to believe how much Mr. Gable spent when he came to get his order for his office. And he wants you to decorate his home as well as his firm." Ally handed her a bottle of water. "You're going to need to keep up your strength if this keeps up."

If this kept up, she was going to be out of business. Sitting down to eat her sandwich, Rayne tried to wrap her head around the inventory she'd just put together. Smiling, she thought she could actually take a day off from this and go to…she had no idea, but she had some free time, and she was damned well going to take it. Now all she had to do was figure out what free time was. Laughing, she called her mom.

"Wanna go shopping for clothes tomorrow?"

Chapter 9

Bronwyn picked up her little girl and just smelled her. There was something so pure about her scent that made her want to bottle it up and keep it with her all day. She heard Sandra come into the nursery and put little Gabriella back in her crib. She turned and smiled at her.

"I love that she smells so good." Sandra nodded. "And I can't thank you enough for watching her this morning. I can't believe that Rayne invited me to go with her and Ally to shop with her today. I've never even thought she liked me all that much."

Sandra snorted. "And why wouldn't she? My goodness, that girl is wonderful, isn't she? And the three of you get along so well that it's almost as if you've known each other since birth."

"I know. I said the same thing to Ryland last night. It's too bad her mom can't go with us, but Ally and I will make sure she comes home with something more than jeans and tee shirts. Do you suppose she has a single skirt or dress?"

"Doubtful. She strikes me as the buy-what-I-need-only sort of girl. And she's been struggling so much to make a name for herself that I'm thrilled she's taking this time. Ally said she got so much done yesterday that people have to move gently through the shop

to get around. I wonder what happened to give her all that energy."
Bronwyn only smiled.

She knew that she'd been changed. Ryland had felt it the moment that the conversion was complete. She'd felt it as well but hadn't known what it had meant until he told her. Rayne was now a cat like her mate was. But they had decided to wait until they were told. Ally had called her yesterday morning to let her know that it had happened as well and that Rayne had so much energy right then that she'd not been able to break her concentration. Ally had smelled it on her. And now she was going to see her too.

When Ally came in the kitchen door, she had Rayne with her. Bronwyn could see the difference in her immediately, and so did Sandra. When she asked to hug her, Bronwyn knew a moment of panic, afraid that she'd hurt her. But Sandra wrapped her arms around her and hugged her tightly without any problems.

"I guess you know, huh?" They all nodded. "I wasn't sure how this worked until I asked Neal this morning. He said that you'd be able to smell it. I think this is really weird just so you know. Having people smell different things about me. But I guess I'm supposed to let you know that we did it willingly. But I'm also sure you know that he wouldn't have been able to force me into anything either."

Rayne flushed and took the glass of tea that Sandra handed her as she explained. "You're going to be fine, and so you know, not everyone can smell you like we can. You'll be able to do it as well when you want. And you're going to remember the scents once you find them."

They left a few minutes later, all three of them loading in the limo that Ryland had sent back for them. He'd told her that they should ride in style today and have fun. He'd also told her to make sure that she spent a great deal of money on the sexy lingerie that he loved to take off her.

"I just thought we'd go to Wally World and maybe grab a burger for lunch." Bronwyn almost felt sorry for Rayne as she sat on the leather seats. "This is way more than is necessary to pick up a few pairs of underwear and some jeans."

"Yes, it is," Ally told her. "That's why we're not going there. We're going to go to the shops in the Howard District and shop there. And I've made us reservations at the Charleston. We're going to be decadent today."

Rayne started to speak, but Bronwyn cut her off. "Don't you dare say you can't afford this. I know for a fact that you have a nice bank account and also credit cards that Neal gave you yesterday. He called me to ask me if he should put Morrow or Golden, and I suggested Golden. Now, we're going to have fun, spend a shit ton of money, and go try on each purchase for our mates. Deal?"

She didn't look as if she was going to agree, but in the end, Ally bullied her into it. When the limo pulled up in front of the first line of shops, they all poured out and walked into the first one they came to. This also happened to be the one she needed to go to.

The store was simply called "*Mine.*" A werewolf owned the stop and had gotten the name of her shop from her mate, who was forever telling her she was his. And Ryland had become a big fan of the word too. Smiling, she looked at Ally and Rayne's faces and could see that neither of them had ever been in here before.

"She's really creative, isn't she?" Then Bronwyn laughed. "I guess that's an understatement. But I love this place and the way the things I buy here make me feel. And the way Ryland looks at me when I wear them for him."

It took some talking, but they finally got Rayne to try on one of the little outfits. *Mine* catered to the fun and sexy rather than just the sexy. She had a whole collection of naughty costumes as well as a selection of things for the more advanced sexual partners. Bronwyn had been toying with the idea of getting a few things from this area for a few weeks now and was looking at them when Ally walked up beside her.

"Do you use this stuff?" Bronwyn shook her head. "Me either. I bet it would be fun, but...I'm not sure my body can take much more fun from Alistair. He's an animal."

They both turned when Rayne came out of the dressing room dressed as the Indian that they could see that she was. The little dress fit her like it had been molded to her body, and the boots, very high heeled, made her legs look incredibly long and sleek. Bronwyn knew that if she didn't buy this for Neal, she was going to and give it to him. Christ, she looked phenomenal.

"It's...I feel pretty." Rayne smiled at her as she turned to the mirrors behind her. "I dressed up once as an Indian princess when I was a child, but this.... This is going to make Neal beg."

They all laughed, and as she changed back into her street clothes, they started to gather up the things they had come for. When Bronwyn wandered back over to the toy section, Rayne came with her this time.

"Do you and Ryland play?" She shook her head, suddenly embarrassed. "Neal and I are starting to figure this out. We're not what's called hardcore or anything, but it's kind of fun to explore. You should get this."

She handed her the feather and looked at her. "I'm pretty sure that dusting isn't what I had in mind when I thought about this."

"No, but it's very erotic when used in the right places, on either of you. And it doesn't tickle after a while. It's almost painful when he or you get into it." She also handed her a pair of silk ties. "Use these while you use the feather on him. I swear to you he'll thank you. And you'll thank me."

She did it. She purchased both the feather and the silk scarves, as well as a maid outfit for her. Who knew? She might enjoy dusting after all. They moved to the next stop after unloading all their purchases in the back of the limo. Bronwyn was just entering the large dressing room when she felt the man enter the shop.

"He's in the middle of the store." Rayne's voice seemed to drift over her. *"He is here for you but not to hurt. Well, not really to hurt you, but he needs to see you. He thinks he knows you."*

"How do you know that?" She pulled her clothes on, ready to leap from the room if he hurt anyone in there. Once was quite enough, and she couldn't protect her family if she was half-naked behind a closed door.

"Plants are not the only thing I can do, Bronwyn. I'm pretty adept at taking care of myself as well as those I've come to be friends with." She smiled at the sarcasm in Rayne's voice. *"He has a gun, though I don't think he thinks of it as a weapon so much as something to intimidate people with. I doubt very much if he's ever fired it other than to qualify with it."*

She started to step out of the room when Rayne told her to stop. She waited for several seconds for her to tell her why when she heard her talking to the man. She was arguing with him more than conversing.

"You did too take my wallet. I felt you touch me, and you have it." Bronwyn peeked out of the crack in the door jam. "I want you to give it back to me right now."

"I don't know what you're talking about. I never touched you or anything on you." The manager made his way over to them when Rayne turned on him.

"I want you to search him. He's taken my wallet, and I want it back. What sort of store is this that women are preyed upon like this? I want him arrested." Rayne looked back at her and winked.

She was enjoying this entirely too much. And, for that matter, so was Bronwyn.

The manager convinced the man to empty his pocket to prove he hadn't taken her wallet. But when it appeared in his things, Rayne went into overdrive. She was shouting at the top of her lungs about her things when Ally slipped into the room with her. She handed her the man's wallet as well as his identification. Both of them.

"She did this to get me information." Ally shrugged. "Does she know that I could have gotten it with a sweep of his mind?"

"Probably, but she wants you to keep the ID. She said it might come in handy soon. She said to tell you that you have your blouse buttoned wrong too." Bronwyn looked down and saw that she was indeed buttoned wrong. She glared at the closed door at the woman on the other side and wondered how she'd known that he had this on him and what it meant.

Over lunch at Charleston, she asked her. "You smell like it. The identification, I mean. You carry the same scent as was on him. Not as strong as he does, but I can smell it."

She tried to think what she meant when she looked down at the badge in her hand. When it occurred to her what Rayne had meant, she paled. It was a lab, one like she'd been to. One where she'd been enhanced to be what she was today. Her fear of Cunningham was unwarranted as he was dead, but she was no less afraid.

"He had been in a hospital, I thought, when I first smelled him. Then when I looked into his mind, I saw a hospital setting and nothing more, so I didn't really put anything together with him. He's been to a bio lab like the one that Cunningham had created, the one that changed me into what I am today, right?" Rayne handed her something else after telling her she had no idea. "What's this?"

"I don't know a great deal about maps, really, but I believe those will take you where he might have been." Bronwyn looked at them and nodded. But the *address,* so to speak, wasn't complete. The last number was smudged so badly that she couldn't make it out.

"Bronwyn, is it another lab? Like the one you were telling me about?" She nodded at Ally. "If that's true, then the government is funding it. It has the CIA's stamp on the back of the badge. You don't think they're trying to find you, do you?"

"I think so. I don't...I think that they've found me." She looked around the room and didn't feel anyone searching for her, and when Rayne grabbed her chin and jerked it around to her, she felt the woman's strength and was startled by it.

"You listen to me, he's not going to find you, and he's certainly not going to take you. Fuck, woman, you're like your own army all by yourself. Buck up, or I'll tell Ryland that you're a big wuss." Anger surged from Rayne to her, and her breath caught. "I told you, I'm not just able to play with flowers. They just calm me. I can do so much more that I'm afraid of myself."

"They've hurt you before." She didn't know why that suddenly occurred to her, but Rayne nodded. "That's why you bought the shop so that no one would find you. No one would hurt you."

"It's mostly why I didn't trust you. I could smell the lab on you the first time you came around. I thought it was because you worked at one, then I realized you'd been tampered with at one like I had." Rayne pulled up her sleeve and showed her a small mark. "There was an implant there. I took it out when I discovered it. Have you looked at yourself?"

"No. I never.... How did you find it? And how did you find it was there?" Rayne pulled her sleeve back down and put her hand on her wrist. "You have to tell me if you know if I have any on me, and how did you find out where it was?"

"You have several on you, and it was a body scan from a friend of mine that found them. And don't fuck around trying to find yours. As soon as the first anything that resembles some sort of scan touches it, the thing alerts someone where you are. I'm pretty sure that whoever put it in you knows not only that you're having lunch here but also that you've just had a baby." Bronwyn tried to think if she'd ever felt anything on her when she looked at Rayne again.

"You never told me. Why? Why, after you figured out that I wasn't your enemy, didn't you tell me?"

"I thought you had already had it removed. I had no idea that you didn't know." Rayne leaned very close to her and Ally. "I have a friend that can remove it for you after we find it, but you have to trust me. He certainly won't hurt you."

Bronwyn nodded. She had something in her that was telling them where she was at all times. They would know her every move, where she was, and what she was. She looked up at Ally when she stood up. Rayne was moving toward the door.

"She said she was making a phone call for us to come out with her after we paid." Ally tossed cash on the table. Bronwyn tried to figure out what to do when Ryland touched her mind.

"You all right?" She told him everything that had just happened, including what had happened with the man in the shop again. *"I'm coming for you. Stay there, and I'll get you."*

"No. I don't...Rayne said that whatever is in me knows everything. She is calling her friend to have it removed. I think I want to get this taken care of before I go near you or the baby right now. I know it sounds stupid because they know so much already, but I need to get this thing if there is one, removed now."

"I don't like this." She told him she didn't either. *"But I*

understand. Keep me informed, okay, love? I'm afraid for you."

"I'll be fine. I know it. Rayne is...she's so much more than we thought, Ryland. And she's been to a lab as well."

~~~

Peter wasn't happy with her, and she didn't blame him. But he was her only hope of getting this fixed. Rayne stepped into the large warehouse and whistled once. Bronwyn wasn't a whiny idiot anymore, which helped her a great deal.

"You do know that I can read your mind, right?" Rayne smiled and nodded at Bronwyn. "And I'll have you know that I've never been a whiny idiot once in my entire life. And as much as I'd like to hurt you right now, I'm pretty sure you can hold your own with me, and I'm too stressed to tangle with you."

Rayne looked at Ally, who nodded. "You have been, sort of. But I completely understand. You're under a great deal of stress and all, and you've just had a lovely baby. Not to mention you've been a little on the quiet side. Not that it's a bad thing but sort of freaky."

Rayne laughed. Ally was very sharp, and a great deal of fun, but Bronwyn was amazing and hard. For their differences, she loved them both dearly. The returned whistle had her moving along the shadows of the empty building.

"I should probably mention that Peter is a vampire. A very old and very strong one. He won't hurt you, but he will ask you for payment. I'll take care of it." Rayne felt his quiet laughter as she spoke. "He's also a pain in the ass more than most humans I know."

"I resent that, Miss Morrow." He sniffed the air around them. "Or should I say, Mrs. Tiger? Hmmm, your blood will be tastier than ever. If I was ever invited to drink from you."

"Behave, or I won't give you what I've brought you." He

moved out of the darkness and revealed himself to them. "Peter, these are my friends and sisters-in-law, Bronwyn Golden and Ally Golden. Bronwyn is the one that needs your help."

"Hum, enhanced, aren't you, my dear?" He walked around them but moved closest to Bronwyn. "You're really marked by the man who created you. I smell four…no six markers on you. I will need more than our usual payment, Mrs. Tiger."

She nodded, and when Bronwyn started to protest, she told her to be quiet. *"He's my friend, and we have an arrangement. It's not what you think. I swear. You said you'd trust me, and I need you to. This is as important for him as it is for you."*

"Come along with me then. I will need you to be naked. I'm not going to harm you in any way, but some of the markers are in very dark places, and as I will need to move quickly to get them all, you'll need to stand perfectly still when I work." Rayne looked at Bronwyn when she didn't move. "You didn't tell her, did you, my dear?"

She hadn't wanted to scare her. But she had to tell her now. "There were several in me as well. Peter had done this sort of thing before, and he knew what would happen once the first one was removed. He has to take them all quickly, or you'll both die."

"Die? Die how? You can't mean that they'll start to poison me as soon as the first one is removed, do you?" Rayne shook her head. "Well, what can be worse than that?"

"You'll explode. They're set to detonate when the first one is touched. Peter will remove them from you with his teeth, biting open your flesh and removing them so fast there won't be time for them to go off before he gets them all out of you." Bronwyn staggered slightly. "When he's finished, I'll heal you because he will need to feed immediately to cure the poison of your blood from his."

"She dies, and I will hunt you down and kill you slowly." She didn't acknowledge Ryland when he touched her mind. *"You so much as get her injured, and I won't stop until you're suffering like you've never suffered before."*

"You think this is helping me? Do you have any idea what this is going to cost me to help her heal? What you have planned for me will be nothing compared to what I have to do." She took a deep breath before continuing. *"You stay the fuck out of my mind for the next hour, or so help me, I will hurt you in ways you've never dreamed of. And trust me, I can do things to you that your poor daughter will even cringe from the sight of you."*

He was still there in the back of her mind, as was Neal. She told him that she had to do this and to contact her mom and have her at her apartment as soon as she could. She watched as Bronwyn took off her clothes and stood still while Peter arranged her. As soon as Bronwyn nodded that she was ready, Peter lunged at her. It was over in seconds, and her work started immediately. She was glad now that she'd eaten a hardy lunch.

The first explosion went off just as she was touching Bronwyn over the first wound. The others, seven in total, had gone off all at once. Peter was very good at this, as neither he nor Bronwyn was harmed by them. As soon as the first wound was healed, Rayne moved her to the floor and finished the healing her body.

It wasn't like with the flowers that she repaired, but human flesh as well as tiger and all the other animals that she had buried deep within her. They all needed her to seal the wounds but also to heal the places where the small markers had been placed in the muscle. Rayne gave the wounds all she was and a little extra so that Bronwyn would be as strong as before. As she closed the last wound, this one deep in her throat, Rayne contacted Neal again.

"I'll be there soon, tell her." She closed her eyes only to open

them as Peter stood before her. "I have brought you the seeds of life. Do you know how to plant them?"

He nodded. "You have been saving these for me, have you not, my friend? You had a plan to come to me?"

She nodded and drifted away. "My home, if you please. And no detours this time. I'm in no shape to enjoy them."

Chapter 10

"Can't or won't tell me?" Ryland paced again and wanted to strangle the woman who sat so still near her daughter. "I have a right to know what she did that cost her so much. You have to tell me what I'm going to owe her."

"I have explained to you several times already, and frankly, I'm getting sick to death of repeating myself. I cannot tell you what I don't know. She has done this for others before, and all I know is that she must have darkness and rest." She pointed to the door. "You're not giving her the rest she needs by standing over me like a ruler and shouting at me."

Ryland moved out of the room and closed the door quietly behind him. He wanted to slam it but was actually afraid that her she-wolf would do just what she'd threatened him with earlier and castrate him. He moved down to the little kitchen and sat in the chair next to Neal. He'd been tossed out of the bedroom earlier.

"She still won't tell you, huh?" Neal said. Ryland shook his head. "She's like her mom a great deal, I think. Rayne, I mean. Very loyal and stubborn, too, but very protective of her cub. I'm betting our children will be just like her. At least I can only hope so."

"She told me that she was going to castrate me before. I believe her," Ryland said. Neal nodded. "I felt her. Rayne, I felt that she was in a great deal of pain as she healed Bronwyn. Every wound that was inflicted on my mate, she felt on her own body as she healed her. She healed her and took away any pain that she might have felt."

"I know." Neal leaned back in the chair as he spoke. "I think that was something to do with the cats, too, but I couldn't tell. I think whatever that vampire did to Bronwyn affected all her animals, not just her cat. I'm pretty sure Rayne had to heal them all."

"You would be correct in that assumption." Both he and Neal stood when the man that had brought Rayne there was suddenly standing in the room with them. "No need to worry, my dear cats. I have fed well before coming here. I am Peter Oliver. Well, there is much more to my name, but Peter will do for now. And as you have probably guessed, I'm her friend and a vampire. Though not in that order necessarily."

"You bit my wife." Ryland wasn't sure whether to kill the man or thank him. He put out his hand in friendship, knowing that even though she was weak, she was alive. "I owe you so much."

"Nonsense. You owe me nothing. I have been paid and paid well by the one who lies beyond." Peter asked if he could sit, and a chair suddenly appeared when he said that he could. Ryland had had to go to the office to get his and was a little disconcerted when the vamp handed him a bottle of wine. He was looking it over when the man laughed at him.

"It's just what it says it is. My dear miss would have my head on a silver platter if I were to hurt one of hers. Serve it while I get to know you." Two glasses appeared in front of them, and Ryland picked up the wine opener and tried to calm his nerves. This was too strange.

"You've known Rayne long?" Neal took his glass and sniffed it. "This is really nice. Very beautiful." Peter nodded.

"I thank you. And it is from my own stock. And in answer to your question, yes I have known the miss for some time. She is a wonderment, is she not? And so talented. But alas, I understand she hides herself under her flowers now. Safer, I suppose, but a loss to us other paranormals that she has helped." He looked to the room again, and Ryland watched as Neal growled. "I shall not harm her. Not because I cannot but because I will never be able to live if I even try. Her story is one of magic and a giving heart."

"She helped you then." Peter nodded, then looked at them both. Neal sat down his glass and leaned forward. "How? Were you a part of what has happened to her, to Bronwyn?"

"No. I was never caught by those monsters, but I did know a little of them. I had the…unwarranted, I realize that now…but I had a thought that if humans wished to kill each other off by messing with their own kind, then who was I to interfere? But then I met the miss one night when I was…how shall I say…indisposed. She saved my life at the near cost of her own."

Ryland could see that the man's memories were harsh. He looked as if whatever had happened that had given him a look into Rayne had changed him completely. When Peter started talking, his flippant way of speaking disappeared, and what Ryland thought was the real man emerged.

"I'd been stabbed and in a very vital part of my body, nearest to my heart, without actually hitting it. Silver is deadly to my kind, and it was running through me like it was blood I'd just feasted upon. The man that I had chosen that night had—for lack of a better term—murdered me. Or so he had thought. But he hadn't known of the child that hid in the shadows, nor of the power that even as young as she was ran deep under her skin."

"Rayne." He nodded at Neal as he continued.

"Yes, Rayne. But I knew not her name, only felt her power, but she knew who I was and what I could do had I not been dying. As the man who had stabbed me with the silver sword stood over me to remove my head from my shoulder, she moved as silent as the night behind him and touched him. A simple touch of her tiny finger to his bared skin sent the man to his knees, then over until his heart stopped beating and his breaths faded away." Peter produced a plate of cheese and crackers as he continued his story. "She picked up the sword nearly twice her height and broke it. She snapped it over her small knee as if it were nothing more than a toy blade. Then she leaned down to me and offered me, a vampire bleeding to death, she offered her life's blood so that I might live. It was the first sip that told me what she was, and a drink was all it took to heal me, bringing me to the point where I was no longer dying to where I am today. I am a changed man."

"I didn't change you. Every time I hear you tell that story, it gets more and more elaborate and a hell of a lot more farfetched. Either tell it correctly or stop telling it altogether." Ryland stood to offer Rayne his chair, but Neal picked her up and settled her on his lap. The vampire approved, it seemed.

"You are perfectly matched, I think." Peter looked at Karin. "Hello, my lady. How are you this fine evening?" Karin moved into the room, and Ryland stood again, giving his chair to the older woman. She looked tired, but he still kept his more manly parts out of her reach as much as he possibly could. He knew she could be mean when it came to watching over her cub.

"Better now, thanks. You helped her again." Peter waved her off. "You did, and you know it. She should have been down for a few days, not a few hours like she was. I thank you once again."

"Thank you, but she is needed." He looked at Neal, then at Ryland. "A man lurks about your family looking for your queen, the she-tiger that Rayne saved tonight. He is not at all happy that someone has taken her markers away from him. He has contacted the one you stole from today. The badge of destruction will be his downfall."

Rayne snorted, took the large glass from Peter, and drank it down before she spoke. "Stop talking in riddles, or I won't give you the rest of your gift."

The vampire sat up higher in his seat and cocked his head at her. "You have not given me enough already? I have planted what you've given me and expect great things from that. What would you give me that is more than that?"

She laid the Baggie in front of him. He looked at it for a long while before he looked at her. He didn't touch it, but even Ryland could see the need to on his face. Peter put his hands on his lap and held them tightly together.

"Why?" When she didn't answer him, he looked at her and nodded to the Baggie. "Why do you give me a gift I can never give you in return?"

"Your birthday, it was yesterday. I had meant to give it to you then, but I got...sidetracked." Neal laughed, then flushed when Peter asked him what that meant. "Never mind. I give this to you freely and without ties. I give you this gift—"

Peter wrapped his hand over her mouth, barely touching it, and held it there as he stared into her eyes. "Do not finish that unless you mean it. I will not have you do this out of a sense of some obligation that we both know you do not owe me." She took his hand away.

"I give you this gift freely from my heart and with my understanding that it can never be taken back from and never will it be returned. Once given, it is yours forever." She picked up the bag and dumped it into her hand, then put it out to Peter. "You have to take my hand, Peter, or all my hard work has been for nothing."

He nodded and reached out with a trembling hand. When he looked as if he might ask her again if she was sure, she took his hand into hers and repeated the vow.

The table shook, and the glasses on the table slid off to the floor, breaking and spilling wine everywhere. When Karin's chair started to move, Ryland reached for her, not having a clue what was happening, but knowing somehow that it was huge. As suddenly as it started, it stopped. Ryland looked at both Peter and Rayne when they both stood up and hugged. Neal didn't move but watched as the two of them parted.

"What the fuck was that?" Peter looked at him and smiled. "If this is some sort of mating ritual, I'm going to kill you. She's my brother's mate."

"I'm well aware of the relationship between them." Peter stood up and bowed before Rayne, then took Neal into his arms for a hard hug. He turned to him, and Ryland took a step back. "You must hug me, sire. If you do not, it will not work. And I will do almost anything for this to work."

Ryland let him hug him and felt the power from the vampire surge into him. He pulled away before he could figure out what it was and watched as Peter hugged Karin. She was crying when he released her, and then Peter turned to them all.

"I'm a free man. Free of the night that is. The soil that she gave me is the dirt that my maker gave her. Without it, I would be a walker of the night forever. The gift that she's given me is the ability to walk during the daylight hours." Ryland looked at Rayne, then at Peter. "It is by far the best gift she could have given me."

"Dirt makes you a day walker?" Rayne shook her head and took his hand in hers, still covered in the dirt. His arm vibrated with the power there, so strong that he felt dizzy from it. He looked at her.

"Feel it, Ryland? It's from a vampire as old as this world is and then some. He is the first, the very first vampire to come here. He made Peter in another world where others like him roam the realm and rule, a place where they both come from. When I contacted him,…he asked me for one thing and one thing only, and that was to make him accept this gift in the name of love." She put her hand behind her when he stared at her. "I never meant for you to be involved in this. I only knew that because of what I am, I'm the only being that could have given him this. And Peter would be the only man, vampire or not, that I would gladly do all this over again for. He's my dearest friend."

Ryland nodded. He wasn't sure how he felt and wasn't really sure what to say to her, but he knew that having a vampire so close all the time was dangerous. Vampires loved shifter blood, and he had a family to protect. Ryland didn't want to hurt her. Rayne had come to mean a great deal to him and his family. But he would hurt her by confessing that he didn't want the man around them. Ever. So Ryland left and was out the door before he could say anything that would hurt Rayne more. Leaving and hurting her would be better than saying how he really felt.

~~~

"I'll go get him," Neal said. Rayne shook her head and smiled. "He hurt you. There was no cause for that. Let me go get him so he can at least apologize for it."

"It's not important. Really. I don't care." She turned to look at Peter, who she was sure knew she was lying. "Viktor wants you to visit him. He said it has been too long, and he misses his child."

"I shall. Will you be all right with your male, my dear? He is quite upset with us." She shrugged. "I can make this right with him if you wish it. I can stay away from you and yours if it would—"

"It wouldn't, and he'll get over it or not. I don't care. I'm just glad that I could do this for you after all this time." He nodded and turned to Neal.

"You have someone special in your heart. I do hope you will keep her safe. The man, Freddy Holden, who comes for the queen, will not care if he gets her or your mate. When he sees this one, he will want her as badly as he does your queen and will stop at nothing to get them. I fear my dear friend will not go down easy this time, either of them."

"You have my word on it that I will do everything within my power to keep them both safe." Peter nodded, then turned to her mom.

"You, I love, my dearest heart. Why do you not just shake off this town and come with me? I travel to the high mountains and to see magic at his purest form in a vampire." He wiggled his brows at her, and she laughed. Rayne loved her mom's laughter.

"You know I can't. I need to have me some grandchildren someday soon, and being with you would cramp my style as a doddering old woman." He kissed her cheek before turning to her.

"You will be safe?" She nodded. "You know just how to contact me. I will be here for you. I owe you so much."

When he was gone, Rayne went to the showroom to see what had happened while she'd been gone. Things had sold, and a great deal of the inventory that she'd finished up just the day before was sitting with "sold" tags on it and even more sitting with "hold" on it. She thought about the things she'd purchased and wondered where they were. She turned to Neal when he stepped up behind her.

"He'll come around." She knew he was hoping that, so she didn't say anything. She took the receipts for the day and was astonished by the sales, but some of the thrill was gone now. She handed them to Neal.

"I'm really tired. I was wondering if you cared if I stayed here tonight. I want to get some things finished up for the weekend, and I have…I have some big projects that I want to get a start on soon." He nodded at her, and she felt her heart crush a little more. "Then I'll see you soon?"

"I'm not going anywhere that you're not, Rayne. I thought you'd figured that out by now." She started to shake her head, and he held her face in his hands. "I love you. With all my heart, I love you dearly. And if you work, I help you. If I need you, I know that you'll help me in the same way. We're together forever."

"But I have a friend who's a vampire. Doesn't that sicken you? I know what your kind thinks about his. You hate him for what he might—" He put his hand over her mouth much like Peter had.

"Not my kind, Rayne, but our kind. You and I are the same. You just happen to have a little more, but we're the same kind of beings. We both are tigers. And if Ryland doesn't understand what you did for that man, then fuck him. He's a small-minded prick if he can't see that." She laughed and went to him. "That's my girl. I love you."

"And I love you too. But Peter won't hurt him. Not because I asked him not to, but because he really is a changed man. He was nearly rogue when I found him. That's the real reason he was being killed. But the moment I saved him he…." Rayne turned around and looked out into the waning evening. "Do you know that in order for him to have lived as long as he has, how much he's seen? What he's had to endure, to go through just to survive? So much of it, I suppose it must have made him overwhelmed and feeling like he'd had enough."

She walked to the large work area and saw the stacks of soil as well as two carts of flowers. On the new wall that Ally had asked if she could put up, there were orders hanging. Rayne took a step closer to read some of them. Orders, some of them large, others just a few herbs put into a cup, were stacked in neat rows for her to work. She looked at Neal when he sat down in the chair she'd been using as a work chair since she'd opened.

"Neal, I'm hungry." He nodded. "I mean really hungry. What do you think we can do? I mean now, what can we do now?"

He stood and moved toward her, and when he was within inches of her, he touched her shoulder just under her shirt collar. She held her breath as he moved his mouth along the same path. Her cat purred, and he lifted his head to look down at her before he touched his mouth to hers. The kiss was long and felt as if he'd touched her with all of him

"I saw the things you bought today. The thought of you dressing in that little outfit had my cock aching to join you in your bed." He slid his tongue over her lips. "And those shoes you bought to wear with it. I want to bend you over one of these tables with you just wearing them and fuck you from behind."

"I'd like that too." She tore the buttons open on his shirt and untied his tie. "But for now, I just need you to feed me."

After having him sit down, she tied his hands to the chair. He was going to enjoy this, she thought. When she knelt between his legs, he opened them for her, and she moved closer to him. She unbuckled his belt and leaned in, and swirled her tongue in his navel. His hiss of approval made her wetter.

When she freed his cock, she licked the tip, then blew across him. He lifted his hips from the chair, and she pressed him back down. Shaking her head, she pulled his pants down to his calves and told him to behave.

"I want to play with you." He nodded. "You might not like this as much as you think you might. I'm not going to give you what you want until I have just what I want."

"You take what you want, and then when you've had your fill, I'll take what I want." She licked his cock again, and he moaned. "I'm not going to survive this, am I?"

"I don't know. Do you want to?" He nodded. "I can make this very hard for you. Harder than you are right now."

"I'm yours. Christ, I'm all yours." She took him into her mouth and twirled her tongue all around his crown. She felt him strain at the tie around him, but he didn't break it. When she leaned back, she took off her bra and then stood up to take off her jeans and panties. Moving closer to him, so his face was where she wanted it, she told him to eat her.

He ate at her so hard and so wonderfully that she nearly forgot that she was running the show. Taking a step back, she nearly went back to him when he growled at her. His command for her to come back to him almost had her begging him to let her come, but she took another step back and held her ground. She only hoped she didn't regret making him so close, only to pull back.

"I'm going to have to punish you for that. I told you that I was going to play. We do things my way." He growled again, and she felt her pussy tighten. If he kept this up, she was going to give in. Then she smiled.

"Watch me, Neal." Sliding her hands down her waist to her hips, she moved her fingers over her mound just above her slit. When she slid her fingers past the wet curls, she moaned and heard him do the same. She'd never done anything like this before and opened her eyes to tell him so when she saw his face. He looked like he was ready to break free and take her to the floor. Lifting her fingers to her mouth, she licked them and then looked at him.

"Are you ready for me?" His growl rolled over her body. "I'm going to suck you until you come. Then I'm going to ride you until I do. Will you be able to come quickly, Neal? I'm in pain. I need to come so badly."

"Let me eat you again. Let me lick your clit until you flood my mouth." She hardly recognized his voice. It was so thick with need, but she shook her head. "When you touch me with your mouth, I'm going to come. I'm going to hold you over me as I fuck that mouth of yours until I'm empty."

She took him into her mouth by bending over him. The sound to her right startled her, and she looked at the chair arm where he'd broken it off, and he curled his hand in her hair and fucked her. She gagged twice, but it didn't seem to matter because the next time he pulled her down, he roared out his release. Before she could move back from him when she thought him to be empty, he stood up and jerked her around so that she was bent over the chair he'd been sitting in.

"Hold on." She wrapped her hands into the back of it, and he slammed deep into her pussy. "Come. Christ, come now. I want to fill you again."

Moving her hand to her pussy, she slid it along her clit in hard and quick moments like he was doing behind her. Every time he pulled to the tip and jerked her back to meet him, she felt his balls slap against her. When he moved his finger over hers and slid both his and hers into her, she felt his cock move like a piston. Her climax at these new sensations had him jerking her upright. As he fucked her with his fingers and cock, she cupped her breasts and pulled hard on her nipples. His command for her to come sent her over the edge twice more until he leaned over her and took her again. As soon as he sank his canines into her neck, she cried out, this time falling over the edge of darkness. Christ, he was going to kill her.

Chapter 11

Frederick Holden looked at the idiot in front of him. When he'd figured out that Pierce had found his prey when none of his others had been able to, Fredrick wanted to strangle the man after he congratulated him on a job well done. But Pierce had made sure that others knew he was there, and Fredrick couldn't simply kill him and mark it off as something that just happened to men like him. He had to have a better plan. Or at least one that didn't involve him getting his hands dirty by spilling the blood of a federal agent.

"She lives outside of town with some rich guy. I believe they're married now, but when she'd moved here, she wasn't. And there's a kid." He looked up at him sharply, and the man moved back in his chair. "A little girl about a week old. I don't have that for sure, but there was an announcement in the paper a few days ago. I hadn't had a chance to connect her with the baby yet."

"Did you see this child? And why would you take the word of a small assed paper like a town this size would print? These places can barely get the names right in big articles, much less the little shit like a birth of a baby." Pierce shook his head, then nodded. "Well, which is it you, fool? I don't have time for your games."

"I've not seen it, but I know it's hers. There was a thing in the paper about her having it on the side of the road. Had to have it delivered by some chick that owns the local flower shop." Frederick nearly came out of his chair then. "Flower shop, you say? What's the name of the owner? Where is it?"

"Out off route forty-three. She's only part-owner and her name…?" He looked at his notes. "I don't think I remember that. It's probably in the article I have in my file."

He stood up, but Fredrick told him to sit. He sent one of the flunkies that were forever underfoot to get this supposed file. Pierce said it was in his hotel room on the table. "I've been keeping notes on everything that I find out about this Bronwyn. She's a real nice lady from all accounts."

He'd just bet she was. She hadn't been when he'd had her oh so long ago. And now this new development nearly had him pulling out his dick and doing a celebratory jerk off. Fredrick laughed to himself, thinking what the fuck in front of him would do if he did that. Or if he told him the only way he could get off was to masturbate with blood, and he didn't care whose it was, his or one of the many that had died for him.

"Good notes, you say? Well, I don't see that. Except for the fact that you can't remember the name of the bitch that whelped her brat or the name of the shop that she is supposed to own, you got some drivel about her being nice. What the fuck kind of notes are you keeping if they're so half-assed?" Pierce nearly let go of his well-known control over his temper. Fredrick was willing to bet the man had never had an erection that his fucking wife didn't shrivel up with just the sound of her voice. He'd met her before and knew that she had a voice that would cut a glacier in two.

"I have been trying to get in to see Mrs. Golden but haven't had any luck. Just yesterday, I followed her into a shop with two other women. When I went in to speak to her, one of them accused me of stealing her wallet. I have never done such a thing. She put it on me is what she did." Fredrick looked at Pierce.

"Are you saying she planted her wallet on you so you could what? Buy something for yourself?" He shook his head and mumbled something. When he was asked to repeat it, all the blood in his body seemed to freeze.

"I said I think it was to steal my identification. Both were missing when I got out to the car. I already reported it stolen and should receive my new badge any time now." Frederick asked him which one. "The one at my work. I guess I should have said something to the lab, but there wasn't any reason to. I'd gotten in without it and wasn't even sure why they had issued me one."

"You've been to the lab?" Pierce nodded. "When? When did you go there, and, better yet, how did you find it?"

"I'd found the longitude and latitude for it among the things that Cunningham's wife gave me a few months ago. And I had done a little digging on my own to find out as much information as I could because there was something about her story that made me…can you imagine if this woman can really change into a cat, what we can use it for?"

"Bronwyn can change into a cat or any other thing she wants to. She has the ability to do whatever she wants because I gave Cunningham the ways and means to give it to her. And you know entirely too much." He pulled out his gun and shot the man in the head. "And now you don't."

The next thing on his list of fuck-ups to take care of was to find this nephew of Pierce's and find out just how much he knew. Probably a great deal less than Pierce did, but like all good snoops, he had to go too. When he found his prey, he wanted her all to himself this time. No more fucking around.

His lab had been his secret. He had had it built with Bronwyn in mind. She wasn't going to get away this time, and neither was his little plaything, Rayne, if this was her. He had no doubt it was because she had had a passion for growing things. To have them both together…he was having a hard time keeping his dick in his pants as he looked at the blood splatter on the wall behind Pierce.

He picked up the phone, having just remembered where Pierce had said he'd gotten the address. "Number one-seven needs to be terminated. I don't care how it looks when it's done so long as she can't be traced back to me."

"Yes, sir." The line disconnected, and he sat back. He had no doubt that within the next ten minutes or so, Mrs. Cunningham would have met with a horrible accident, leaving her two small children orphans.

Frederick sat back and waited for the file to come to him and for someone to come and clean up Pierce's mess. The man had moved ahead of the game much too quickly and hadn't done what he'd been told to do. He was going to have to have a little talk with Brads, Pierce's work buddy, too when he got back. He was supposed to tell him to give it up and forget about the box of shit from the Cunningham woman. Well, he was going to have to see to it that he didn't fuck up again. Laughing, he picked up his phone again.

"Kill Brads." This was met with another *yes sir,* and he knew then that the matter was taken care of. When the call came to him five minutes later that one-seven had committed suicide, he smiled. One down and two to go. But he had a feeling that little Bobby was going to be a walk in the park to take out.

~~~

Neal sat at his desk for nearly an hour before he was ready to say fuck it and go to the shop. He'd been late coming in, and no one seemed to notice, and now he was simply sitting there with his computer screen gone to black, and he couldn't remember the first thing about what he'd been doing before that. When his phone rang, he nearly didn't answer it.

"Neal Golden." He smiled when his mother laughed. "See, I took your advice and started answering it with the name you slaved over."

"You're a good boy. But I need something from you. You know that lovely little planter that I bought from Rayne? The one with all those purple flowers in it?"

"Hydrangeas." He'd been getting really good at naming the flowers too. "What about it? You didn't forget to water it, did you?"

"Good heavens, no. How would that look if my future daughter-in-law gave me instructions on how to keep it alive and I couldn't? How would that look to the flower club I chair too? No, I need another one. But in pinks. I think I saw that she had one in pink there, didn't I?"

"If she doesn't, I'm sure she'll make you one. Did you need it taken somewhere?" She gave him the name of a friend of her daughter, and he wrote it down.

"She just had a baby girl, and I thought what a lovely gift to give her. Rayne told me that they can live for a very long time with proper care. And I'm sure it will get good care where it's going." He assured her he'd ask her. "Also, when are you getting married? I would have thought by now you would have at least asked her. Goodness, son, do you need to take lessons from your brothers?"

"No." He pulled the ring box out of his pocket and opened it. "I was going to do it last night, but she had company, and then later, we had to finish up some orders." And he wasn't going to tell his mom, but he'd been distracted by her naked body while she'd filled pot after pot with soil so that all she had to do today was fill them with plants. He put the ring away.

"I'm going to meet her after she closes up tonight. Then we're going to go and look for her a car. I didn't even know she didn't own one until last night." He looked up when May walked in. "I have to go, Mom. I need to get out on time, and I still have a ton of work to do."

"You might want to rethink that." May shut the door behind her. "There's a man in the lobby that says he has to see you. He said that he thinks someone is trying to kill him, and since your brother Ryland is tied up in meetings, he said you'd have to see him. His name is Bobby Smyth. He said his uncle, Sheldon Pierce, hadn't contacted him for several hours, and he should have. He said that Pierce works for the CIA and has been trying to contact Bronwyn."

"Where is he now?" She told him near the security desk. "I'm going to call Brock and let him know what's going on and have him meet me down there. I'm not sure what this guy thinks an accountant is going to help him with, but maybe he needs something else."

She nodded as he reached for the phone as she went out, leaving the door open. He could hear her speaking to someone and realized it was Stan, telling him to hold Mr. Smyth until she could contact someone. May left her desk after hanging up the phone. She told him she was going to see if Ryland had a few minutes to spare. Brock answered on the first ring.

Neal told him everything that May had told him. "I'm going down to see what I can figure out. Can you come down too?"

"Sure. Give me two minutes, and we'll go together. I think Ryland and Alistair are going too. Both of them are with me." Neal nodded and walked to his door just as his cell phone rang. He smiled as he answered it.

"Don't speak. Just listen to me. I've been taken from my shop, and my mom is hurt. Bronwyn is with me, and she's hurt but not badly. I can't heal her until I see what this mad man has in store for us. I think he's taking us to the address we'd found." He felt the finger of fear run up his spine as Rayne whispered to him.

"Leave the phone on if you have to. I'll find you." He moved to the hall just as his brothers were coming to him. They were laughing, and he was so afraid that he wanted to drop to his knees and beg them for help.

"Go to the shop. The baby is there. I'm so worried for her. My mom…will you please see that she's taken care of too? He…he just shot her." The signal seemed to drop for a few minutes, and he caught himself screaming for her. He looked at Ryland when the line went dead.

"We have to get to the shop. Someone has taken them. Both of them. Rayne said that the baby was at the shop and that her mom is hurt." All three of them took off to the stairs knowing that they could run down them faster than waiting on the elevator.

Brock said he'd deal with the man as the two of them took off for the garage. Ryland's car was closer, so they got in it and tore out of the underground area as if their lives depended on it. Neal supposed, in a way, it did.

"Who took them, did she say?" He said that she hadn't. "I'm going to kill the son of a bitch when we find him."

They pulled into the parking area just as the police did. The alarm had been pulled, they'd said, and had asked for them to wait. Ryland nearly knocked the first man down, getting inside when it was cleared.

The baby was crying, or they might not have found her. She had been hidden deep in one of the pots that had been in the work room with an empty soil bag over the top of it. When Ryland picked her up and held her to him, it was all Neal could to do stand up with him. He looked at his brother as he cooed at his little girl.

"She smells like Rayne," he told him softly. "She was the last person to hold her, so she hid her from whoever came here. I don't know what happened here, but your mate saved my daughter again."

It took them nearly ten minutes to find Karin, but she'd not been so lucky. Her arm was broken in two places, and she had lost a great deal of blood. When she opened her eyes to look at him as she was being loaded into an ambulance, Neal had to lean very close to hear her.

"He took her. You must find her." He nodded. "Here is his scent." She uncurled her hand, and he looked down at the scrap of material from her and held it to his nose. Her last words to him as she was being closed inside were to contact Peter.

"How do you do that?" He looked at Brock as he took the material to his nose as well and shrugged at Ryland. "And what sort of help do you suppose he could be? Other than draining us all in our sleep. Or better yet, thanks to your mate, any time of the day or night."

Neal's temper snapped. He jerked his brother up so hard that he startled little Gabriella into waking suddenly. But he didn't let him down. Not even when she started screaming in his brother's arms.

"You'll keep your tongue behind your teeth, or so help me to Christ, I will lay you out beside him when I find the bastard who dared touch what is mine." He gave Ryland a hard shake.

Brock touched his arm. "Let him go. Neal, let him go before you hurt the baby, and then Bronwyn will have your ass."

He let Ryland go and realized that he'd never fought back. He walked away just as he felt the room tighten and there stood the vampire. He bowed before him and looked around.

"Karin said you wanted to talk to me. This is amazing being out in the....What's happened here?"

"Someone took them. Both Rayne and Bronwyn and hurt Karin bad enough that she's lost a great deal of blood and has a few broken bones too. Also, I think they were looking for my baby. I can only imagine what they wanted with an infant, can you?"

"To raise her to breed for them," Peter told Ryland in answer to his question. "I know where they are taking them, but...I cannot get into the building. Someone knew about me and has blocked my kind from entering. Unless someone enters and allows me to come in, I'm afraid all I can assist you with is getting you there."

"Take me there." Before he could make arrangements to drive anywhere with Peter, he was suddenly standing just outside the massive building. "I thought we'd all come together."

He leaned over, feeling sick, when suddenly Brock was there too. When he returned with Ryland as well, Neal could have kissed the man. Ryland hugged the vamp to him.

"I'm sorry. I'm sorrier than I've ever been." Ryland looked at Neal. "Will you forgive me as well? I was...she's all I have, and I was stupid."

"Yes, you were, and an asshole too. You made Rayne cry, and for that, I should knock the shit out of you." Peter laughed at him, and he glared at him. "Well, he is when he wants to be."

"But he is your male." Peter moved to the front of the building and stood still. "She is inside. There is another with her, but I cannot read her, so I can only surmise that it is your female. Rayne is hurt but not badly. The other woman is as well. Again, not badly. What is the plan?"

"There are several men that could help us. How many times can you do this before you have to rest?" Neal looked at Brock with a raised brow. "This is not my first vampire. I know a few of them."

"I can make perhaps five more trips. Less if the person is large. Like the bear at your home, Ryland. Shall I bring him to you?" As soon as Ryland nodded, Peter disappeared only to return with Max. Just as Peter let him go, Max took a swing at him.

"I was having dinner with my family, you fucking asshole. What the fuck did you have to do that for, Peter?" Neal wasn't even surprised to know that the two of them knew each other. "You could have at least said hi to my wife and children before you snatched me from my home like it was an emergency or something."

"It is. Bronwyn and Rayne have been kidnapped, and we think they might have been intent on taking my daughter." Max looked at the building and asked Ryland if the women were inside there. "Yes. I need to get them out."

"You'll need the other cats. The ones the missus got as a streak the first time out. Mike will know how to get 'em here, Jonny quick like if you want them." Max looked at Peter. "You know how to find the rogue cat, don't you?"

Peter made another trip back and brought three of the cats with him. They were hanging on him like ornaments on a tree. When he staggered slightly, Neal helped him sit down.

"I might have overestimated myself a little." Without thought to what might happen, Neal offered him his wrist. "You know what this means, do you not? It means we are about to have the best sex of your life."

Neal jerked his arm back, and Peter fell over laughing. Neal kicked at him, cursing. "Stupid ass, don't you know how serious this is? I was trying to help you, and you make jokes."

He laughed with him and was glad that the old man had done it. It had broken the tension. And he took his first deep breath in hours. He shook his head when Peter continued to laugh for another five minutes or so.

"I am sorry, but had you been able to see your face, you would have...." He took his wrist again and, this time, licked along the vein. "I will only take what I need to help. Nothing more. But we'll have a connection akin to the one that Rayne and I have."

"You help me get them out, and I'll be happy to discuss whatever connection you want. After we get them out." Peter nodded and sank his teeth into his wrist.

There was little pain, but he knew as a supernatural being that the lick he'd given his wrist would deaden the pain. When he lifted his head, Peter looked at him oddly but only told him thanks. By the time the other cats were with them, a dozen total, they were about as ready to storm the castle as they'd ever be. Just as they were about to enter the compound, a large limo pulled up, and a man stepped out.

"That is the man you need to end." Peter nodded to him. "He is Holden, Freddy Holden, and he's a rogue."

Neal turned to look at him. "Rogue, as in vampire? You've got to be kidding me? Who the hell would want a rogue vampire running around with the CIA?"

"One who does not care so long as the job is finished. And he is not a vampire but a human who has no scruples or anything redeeming about him." Peter looked back at the building as he continued. "He is not a good man, as you know, but if we go in there as we are...I believe it is called half-cocked, though I don't understand that term...we will surely get ourselves killed as soon as we enter. He is a man who would kill them rather than have anyone else get his prize. I think we need a plan."

Neal agreed with him. "There's a grove of woods we can meet at over there. I think if we just sit down and think this through, we can get the women out and get them home."

"And the others." They all looked at Mike. "There will be others in there. This lab, it's not unlike the others that your mate and I have been in before. They will have others inside that they are working on, killing, breeding. We need to make sure that they're out as well."

They all nodded. If it was possible to get them all out, they would, but they were going to get their mates out first and foremost. Neal would die if he didn't have Rayne by his side.

Chapter 12

Rayne knew she had to help Bronwyn, but she was afraid if she did, she wouldn't be able to save either of them. Reaching down to touch the other woman, she felt the need to heal course through her. "Fuck it."

Pressing her hands over her, she moved along her body and found why she wasn't waking up. They'd hit her pretty hard in the head, and there was some major damage. Cursing more at the men who had come to her place and took them, she sent all she was into her wound and repaired all the damage. If Bronwyn was half as strong as she thought she was, Rayne thought she would be able to get them both out.

When she opened her eyes twenty minutes later, Rayne could have wept. She leaned down to her and told her not to move. Then she nodded to the camera above them. Bronwyn asked if they had gotten Gabriella.

"No. I heard them coming through the room just after you'd left us and hid her. I put her into a little bit of a sleep to keep her quiet. I'm sorry about that." Bronwyn told her that it was fine so long as her child was. "I called Neal on the cell phone before we were brought inside, knowing that we wouldn't be able to communicate with them after that. They hurt my mom."

"We'll get out." She closed her eyes again, and Rayne walked to the other side of the room. When Bronwyn touched her mind, she nearly screamed. She hadn't realized that she could do that too.

"I'm getting stronger. I'm assuming that you had something to do with that." She told her she had. *"I thank you. When we get out of here and fuck this place up, you and I are going to do some serious shopping. On line. I'm sick of malls and shops where we can get cornered and shot up. That's just fucked up no matter how you look at it."*

Rayne laughed, knowing that's what she'd meant for her to do. It felt good, invigorating, as well as lifting her spirits. She sat down on the bed and looked out into the open lab.

"I've been to one like this before. I think the same man runs it. Do you know a man by the name of Holden?" She told her that she didn't, but that didn't mean she hadn't had contact with him. *"You more than likely had. Some guy I think we both knew helped him run one once before. Cunningham. Him, you do know."*

"Yes. He had a lab not far from here, as a matter of fact. When we went in, it was such a mess. Dead bodies had been stacked in rows in any room they could find a place to put them. Some of them had been in there for so long that it had been difficult to tell what they were, much less who they were." Rayne felt a small twinge of power come over her. *"I'm giving you a little at a time until we're both about even. What you gave me healed me, and...I think you give up a part of yourself when you heal someone, don't you?"*

"Yes, for the most part. I think I get most of my energy from the plants when I...help them, I suppose. It's why I wanted to work with them. No matter what I'm feeling, the first time I touch them, I feel the difference." She leaned back against the wall. *"When they come for us, they're going to want you to tell them about*

your daughter. The man who hit you said that he was to bring her back with him. I think Holden thinks of her as a sort of prize or something. When I was here...they...I was to be used for breeding purposes."

"Me too. They tried to take my eggs, but...well, I'm pretty fucking bad assed when I'm pissed." Rayne laughed at her. *"I'm betting you are, too. Other than the plants, what is your specialty?"*

Before she could answer her, someone came into the lab. She didn't bother standing because, first of all, that would show him she cared and, secondly, she was saving her energy. She glanced at Bronwyn and saw that she'd closed her eyes again. She thought it was a good idea that they thought her too hurt to defend herself for now.

"Well, well, well. We meet again, my dear child. I had heard that you were dead. At least that's what the little tracers said when I asked them. How on earth did you get my markers out without killing yourself?" He had a chair brought to him, and he sat down. He was well away from the cell doors, but she knew if she wanted him, he'd be close enough in a second no matter what he did.

"I'm resourceful. How is it you get fatter every time I see you and still live?" She laughed when he sputtered. "What have you put on? Fifty? Sixty pounds? Must be all that desk work you do. Makes you forget that you need to be in better shape to fuck with me, I'm thinking. Why don't you come a little closer, and I'll show you how resourceful I can be."

"You think you're so brave on the other side of that cell? I can have you shot from here, and we both know that. How many times did I do that before until you got the idea that I mean business? Ten? Fifteen? I'm thinking the latter number."

She laughed at him when he told the man standing next to him to give him his gun. The man hesitated for several seconds until he handed it over. The moment that he touched it, he dropped it and cried out. Rayne wanted to look at Bronwyn but didn't want to give away her being awake.

"You fucking cunt. You'll pay for this." He shook his hand, and she could see the blisters already forming. He'd been burnt.

"He can't shoot you, not if I have to heal you and get us out of here." Bronwyn sounded pissed off. *"Asshole. Yeah, I remember him, but he went by the name of Sandalwood back then. And you're right. He is a fucking tub of lard."*

"Where's the kid?" She looked at him oddly. "I know you know about her having a baby. You delivered the fucking thing. I'm thinking with your power and hers together, that kid has to be amazing."

"I didn't father her baby, you dimwit. I only helped bring it into the world. Where do you get your information from? Your boy Sheldon, or is it his nephew Bobby? Where is that boy, I wonder?" She thanked Bronwyn for the extra information and knew that they had scared Bobby into running where they hadn't found him yet. "You killed poor Sheldon, and now the manhunt is on for the boy. But you won't find him. Want to know why?"

He stood up and came within a foot of the cell. She could have gotten to him before he backed off, but she wanted to give him just enough leeway to hang himself. Or her kill him. It didn't matter to her so long as he was dead.

"You think you're so fucking special, don't you? The little faerie that has her little plants is so bad assed that no one can touch her. But I did, didn't I? I got news for you, bitch, you ain't all that special, and as far as your shop goes, I'm going to take care of that tonight. You're going to be fucking history, just like your shop."

She didn't move. Her shop would be destroyed, and there wasn't a fucking thing she could do about it but mourn the loss.

When she felt Bronwyn touch her mind again, she brushed her off. She was in enough pain right now and didn't want or need any sympathy from her.

"You think that the shop is going to break me, Freddy? Make me just simply roll over and let you have what you want?" She stood up, and he backed up, almost tripping over the chair behind him. "You'd better fucking hope that when we get out of here that I kill you first because if I don't, I'm going to give you to the 'subjects' that you've been playing with. You think they're going to let you go gentle in the night, Freddy boy?"

"Stop calling me that fucking name. I told you before, it's Frederick. And if you can't remember that, then Mr. Holden. Or Master. I like Master." He took a step toward her and backed up again when she stepped toward him. "You're fucking going to beg me to kill you. You and that fucking cunt laying there that just might live until tomorrow will both be dead as soon as I get what I want from you both. And even if I have to kill you myself without a single test, you're not leaving this compound alive."

He was nearly to the door when she said his name. She didn't say another word until he turned, and then she smiled at him. "Wanna take bets on which one of us leaves here in a body bag? Will it be you or me?"

Rayne looked around the lab again and then at the two men standing on the other side of the cell. They were armed with weapons she was sure didn't come from the local gun shop, and the body armor they had on was thick and, she was sure, bulletproof. She didn't care. If she wanted them dead, they would be. She told Bronwyn to cover her face.

The cameras exploded all around the room. The one in her cell stayed on long enough for her to stand up and flip off the thing before she turned her back, and it, too, exploded. She looked over at the two men and smiled. The one on the right looked at his partner, then back at her.

"Boo." When he took a step back, she laughed. "You have five seconds to leave here or so help me, you'll be in twice as many pieces as those cameras. Five, four, three…."

They were gone before she could say two. Rayne turned to Bronwyn. She was sitting up and smiling at her. Blood no longer seeped from the wound at her head, but she did look pale. When she stood up, she reached her hands into the air, and the lab came apart.

Tables bent in half. Glass jars along the walls exploded, and their contents spilled everywhere. Some of it smoked as it hit the tiled floor; some just hardened. The chair that Freddy had been sitting in ended up in the wall about a foot deep, and the cabinets that held things like gloves and gowns rained down on the room as if it was a freak storm. Rayne turned to look at her.

"I'm guessing you're feeling better." Bronwyn nodded and reached for her. "No thanks. Whatever you have might kill me."

She touched her anyway, and Rayne felt as if she had touched a live wire. Crying out with it, she gripped the cell bars as her body adjusted to whatever she'd done to her. When she looked at her again, Bronwyn was smiling.

"Don't ever do that again." She nodded. "I'm fucking serious. That was…fuck, that hurt. You do that to Freddy boy, and he'll piss his pants."

"If I did it to Freddy at all, I won't hold back. And he'd be dead the moment I put my hands on him." Rayne wanted to ask her how much she'd held back but didn't. She wasn't sure she wanted to know if she had held back a lot or just a little. Either way, she felt like she'd been reenergized to the max.

~~~

Bronwyn was trying her best not to be impressed with the little flower girl. She'd taken to calling Rayne that when she and Ryland talked about her. She'd have to rethink that because she could now see she was more than just a person who played in the dirt. Rayne was amazingly strong. And she'd taken her gift like no one ever had before, and she'd taken all of her not a little like she'd told her. Christ, she'd killed men with less.

"If this building is anything like his other labs, there will be a holding area below us. I want you to get out of here and back to your daughter, and I'll—"

"Do you know her name? Her full name?" Rayne looked at her oddly, then shook her head. "It's Gabriella Rayne Golden. We were going to have her middle name be Angel, but we wanted to name her for her godmother."

"You named your daughter after me? Why would you do that? Hang on? Godmother? I can barely take care of me, and you want me to raise your daughter? I think you should rethink that pretty fucking quick." Bronwyn laughed. "I mean, it's a pretty name and all, but sheesh, the kid will be called Stormy Weather for the rest of her life if anyone finds out."

"No, she won't because you'll tell her not to let them and show her how to beat the shit out of the first one who tries." Rayne shook her head. "And I'm not leaving here without you. *We're* going to go to the holding area together, and *we're* going to help those out that can't move, and *we're* going to kill that fucking tub of lard Holden as a team."

She looked down the stairs, then back at her. "You know you sound just like Neal. He gets pissy, too, when I think I can do something all on my own. If I didn't know better, I'd say the two of you were sister and brother and not in-laws."

She thanked her and followed her down the flight of stairs. It took them ten minutes to find the area. Along the way, they opened cell doors as they passed them and helped who they could to their feet. Two were dead, or so close it mattered little, and they found one child on this floor. Handing the little boy off to one of the ones who could walk, they showed them on the map how to leave the building from the basement.

"Nice of him to provide us with a fire escape plan, don't you think?" Rayne nodded as she opened another door. In this cell were three small cubs, wild wolves that had been stolen from their mother too soon and were starving. Going to the refrigerator, she found some meat that was still vacuum sealed and tore it open and tossed it to them. They nearly were too weak to eat. Rayne found a bowl and filled it with some water she'd found too.

"They'll need care." Bronwyn nodded at her. "I have a customer that works at the zoo. Maybe he can make sure they're taken care of. Put them somewhere they can get healthy again or something."

They moved on after handing off the cubs to three of the others that were leaving. When they came to the holding area, a large open area that held larger cages, Bronwyn hesitated.

"I can go in and see if you want to wait here." She nodded at Rayne. "I've not spent as much time in these places as you did, but I know what can happen to people like us."

"He would put me in the smallest cage and not feed me for days on end. And even then, it wasn't fit for eating. I've done things that I thought…." She looked at Rayne. "I have the love of a man that I nearly worship, a daughter that makes me feel like I can conquer the world, and a family that I would die for. But the thought of going back into one of those rooms makes me want to crawl into a corner and whimper."

Rayne stepped into the room, and Bronwyn waited. She stood

there watching her move from cage to cage. When she touched her mind, she had to smile. The girl learned fast.

"You do know that by not coming in here, he wins, right?" She glared at her. *"I'm just saying that the best way to come out on top is to get your ass in here and help me. Besides, you owe me for zapping me."*

Bronwyn touched the door to enter. *"You're a bitch, did you know that? And so you know, what I gave you was everything I have. I didn't hold back. Others have died with only half of what I zapped you with."*

She was laughing when she entered. Rayne looked like she just might hit her, but when she entered the room completely, she nearly turned and ran. The room flooded her with memories and nightmares. Bronwyn took her hand when Rayne touched her.

"No one in here is going to hurt us. They are…for the most part. Most of them have given up anyway and won't be able to leave here on their own, if at all. Listen to them."

Kill me, please. Leave me here to die. Some of them chanted their needs. Others mumbled them. One man was begging them to tell his mate that he loved her, and yet another was asking them to get her out. This wasn't as bad as she'd seen it, but it was horrific. They moved from cage to cage together, putting the weaker ones on gurneys that others had brought. Three men from the upper areas had come down to help, knowing, they said, what was down here.

"There is more, missus." Bronwyn looked at the larger man. "Just beyond. Don't know if they live or not, but there are more of us here."

He led them to the next level down. This was where the worst of it was. Cages hadn't been cleaned for months; animals, most of them only skin and bones, lay in their own shit and urine. There was no hope for some of them, and they seemed to have known it. Two had killed themselves; three were dying. And the rest were so weak it would have taken more than just the five of them to get any of them out.

"We have to leave them until we can get them out with help." Rayne shook her head, and Bronwyn grabbed her when she went to one of the cages. "They'll die if we move them. And if they don't, how do you suppose we get them out of here and to help with all guards waiting for us now? You know as well as I do that we've only gotten this far without encountering them is because we've come down instead of up. If he catches us with these injured, he'll kill us all."

"They're hurt." She nodded at Rayne. "We'll come back for them, you promise? We won't leave even one of them behind even if we have to take them out kicking and screaming?"

Bronwyn knew at that moment that Rayne had left someone behind when she'd escaped before. And she still carried the guilt of it. Bronwyn reached out and touched her head and found the memory.

"He was afraid of slowing you down." Rayne nodded.

"Jimmy. I didn't know his last name, but he was a vamp like Peter. Not as old, but up there. They were using him for his blood, trying to see if they could duplicate his regenerative powers. All they fed him was pig's blood, and he was never strong enough to give them what they wanted. He told me to find some way to escape and to make something of my life, I was all but carrying him by then, and he was slow in moving. All I was able to do until I opened my shop was go from one dead-end job to another. He would have been so ashamed of me."

"Ashamed of you? How the fuck do you figure that? You survived, didn't you? You got your ass out of that dead-end job situation and put yourself out there." She bopped her in the forehead with the palm of her hand. "Get real, woman, you're more than he could have ever hoped you'd be. And let's just say it right now, you're my friend, and that makes you the coolest of them all."

She laughed. "You're insane, do you know that? And I'm glad you're my friend. I don't have a great many…hell, I don't have any, so I thank you."

They left them there. They'd had no choice, really, and as they were leaving, they came across another set of stairs. Before they could move down them, they heard something coming up. Both of them hid in the rooms they'd just come from and waited. The voices drifted up to them before the two men.

"I'm thinking that with both of them here and still breedable, we find someone to fuck them until they have a kid. Think what we can do with an offspring of either of them." It was Freddy; she'd know his voice anywhere.

"Won't work, I'm afraid. They're both cats and can only be impregnated by their mates. Not even artificially impregnating them works without the right sperm." The other man laughed, and Bronwyn looked at Rayne when she whimpered. "Maybe we can find their mates, bring them here, and have them fuck the shit out of them until we get a whole litter of them. Could work, I suppose."

"Yeah, I guess. I guess we have the room, and if we don't, well, we could always reduce our numbers by a few. Especially since we'll have them doing just what we needed in the first place." Freddy cleared the stairwell first and turned back to the other male as he continued. "You should know that I don't know if that fucking cunt Lawrence is gonna make it. That fucking jack wipe hit her hard enough to spill out some of her gray matter."

The man stepped into view and looked right at her. "It seems we've been exposed. Hello, Raynie. Long time no see."

Rayne stepped out from behind the cabinet. "Hello, Jimmy. I thought you were dead. You helped me out of here only to bring me back, and I thought I'd killed you by leaving you behind. That won't happen again."

"Yes. When it looked like you weren't going to cooperate without someone beating you shitless for days at a time," he said with a shrug. "I decided that it would be nice if you lived long enough for me to kill you myself. You always were a sap. And now that I have you right where I want you…well, let's just say that you're going to pay for not offering me your wrist when I asked you for it."

"You always did think the sun rose and set for you. But I got news for you, you're nothing but a blood-sucking prick who is going to regret the day he was made. And you know what? I'm going to be the one that makes you pay."

"Mother fuck," Bronwyn whispered.

Chapter 13

Neal saw them but couldn't quite wrap his mind around what he was seeing. There were.... "Does anyone else see that?"

Ryland turned to look at him, and he pointed to the far side of the lab. There were so many people running toward the tree line that he thought for sure that he was imagining it. Also, he could see that there were wolves, tigers, and panthers, as well as humans. He looked at Ryland when he chuckled.

"Someone is helping them escape," Neal said. Ryland looked at him. "I bet we can guess who might be doing it too. Come on."

They circled the lab and went to the other side. All of them ran toward the people leaving the large facility and helped them as much as they could. Small children were shoved in their hands, while some were lifted by the cats that had come with them and taken deep into the woods. Ryland pulled out his cell phone and called for help.

"They're bringing the clinic with them." Neal nodded as he wrapped one of the injured in his shirt. "Danny said he'd call in everyone he could and have them meet us here. I'm going to call Mom now. See if she can gather up some food and clothing too. I think we're going to need it with all these people."

The beings that hadn't shifted were near naked. Most of them had on underwear so dirty and grimy that they looked a part of their skin. He helped a man whose leg looked to be infected lay down on the ground. He covered him with some leaves, not knowing how else to keep him from being exposed. One of the men who had carried a pair of wolf cubs leaned into him and sniffed.

"You smell like her. She and another woman helped us out. Said we were to run like the gates of hell had been opened and we're being chased. We did, but I'm not so sure some of us will survive it." He looked down at the man he'd been helping and noticed that he'd stopped breathing. "She said that the dead were supposed to have more'n this. We can't be letting that lard man win."

"Lard man?" He figured it out about the same time the man was describing Holden. "She's very brave and smart, my mate. Were they all right when you saw them? The other woman had been hurt badly, I heard."

"They be fine as rain when I saw them. She got herself a foul mouth, she does, when she's getting a man going. Durn near took my ear off when I told her that I wasn't fit to carry them wolves. She said she would tear it off'n me and feed it to'em if I didn't get my bottom in gear." He looked around when Neal did. "That man needs to be kilt like the others been. Nobody should be allow'n to do that to peoples that ain't done a durn thing to him and his."

By the time help arrived, they'd lost three more. One of the pregnant women who'd come out had lost her child, but she'd seemed so relieved by it that no one had told her how sorry they were. She was human and told them that the monster that she was carrying wasn't going to be anything anyone wanted anyway. The "child" had been so deformed that it was difficult to tell what she'd been going to have anyway. She let one of the cubs cuddle up to her while she waited her turn to be helped.

His mom arrived ten minutes later with several trucks following her. She had baskets of clothes that some of the women from her sewing circle had been going to use for scraps. The men who had driven the other vehicles walked around handing out bottled water and warmed soup, cans of soda for the sugar, and candy bars galore.

"What did you do, rob the local convenience store?" She pulled him into her arms, and he held her while she sobbed. "It's going to be okay, Mom. We'll get them out. They sent these others to us, so they can't be far behind."

"Look at these poor people, Neal. How will some of them ever get over this? How did Bronwyn ever survive this?" He held her tighter to him, not mentioning that Rayne had survived this as well. "You must think I'm a ninny for sobbing over this."

"No," he told her. "I've been doing a bit of crying myself. That man over there told me that some of the people still in there couldn't be helped out until a medical team entered. Another told me that he only got out because Rayne and Bronwyn threatened him. I think they're afraid of them."

She looked up at him with tears in her eyes. "Son, there are times when I'm afraid of them myself. And Ally can be just as scary. These women you boys have brought into our family? I would hate to tangle with any of them. Can you imagine what that person in there is going to get coming to him with the two of them working together?" She shivered.

Neal started laughing. And as he told Ryland what mom had said, he started laughing too. Soon most of the people were laughing with them, having met the two women and knowing firsthand what sort of trouble they could be.

He almost felt sorry for the sick bastard that was about to

tangle with a couple of the meanest cats he knew. When he was finished helping the last few of the survivors into one of the many vehicles that had come across rough terrain to help out, he looked stood next to Ryland and Peter, who stood staring at the lab.

"If we go in now, we risk getting the others hurt and probably the two of them. If we don't, then we can't help them." Ryland looked at him. "I just don't want to get them hurt either way."

"We still don't have a plan. And there are more coming out still." Two men and a woman came toward them. "And the way these people are still coming out makes me think that either the assholes running this place don't know they're getting out, or they just don't have the manpower it takes to chase them down."

"Or they could be dead." Both he and Ryland shook their heads at Peter. "I do not mean the women. What I mean are the ones that work there. They have to be scrambling around, trying to get to safety. I would be if I were them."

"What do you think we should do, Neal? Go after them by ourselves the way these people are coming out, or do we go through the front doors like we'd planned and take them all on at once?"

"Why not both?" Neal pointed to where another person was coming from. "You and I could go there, where we're both pretty sure our mates are, while the rest go in the front doors and take them all out. We don't have to worry so much about getting the innocent hurt. I'm reasonably sure that most of them have made it to us anyway. And the few that had to remain behind can be taken care of when we get inside and take care of this place."

It took them ten minutes to devise the plan. Mike and his team were going to go in the front while he and Ryland went in the back. Mike wasn't thrilled about the plan, but he knew it was the best way to get everyone else out. But he'd warned him before he left them.

"Destroy everything. And once you find the addresses for those that are working here, we'll make sure everything they might have taken home is destroyed as well. We want to kill this disease before it spreads to everyone." Neal nodded, and Mike shook him. "I'm dead serious. If you don't get everything, then you might as well invest in the next lab because it's going to happen."

He and Ryland were running down the same path that the others had used when the first shot rang out. When he and his brother made it to the building, they heard shots being fired on the other side. Neal looked at Ryland, and as one, they stripped down. Their cats would have a better chance of taking anyone on than they would. As their tigers, they moved into the building, hoping that their mates were going to be found soon.

~~~

They were only going to get out if they worked together. Rayne stepped near Bronwyn and reached for her hand. Power surged between them like an electrical wire. When Jimmy stepped toward them, she raised her hand in warning.

"I'm no longer the little kid you kidnapped, Jimmy. I'm a grown woman who has come into her power. I would just walk away if I were you." He grinned at her in the condescending way he had about him. "You're not very smart, are you?"

"Oh, I wouldn't say that. I've been able to elude the authorities for most of my vampire life. I've managed to become one of the richest men in the world and have a great deal to show for it." He waved around the room they were still in. "Like this lab. It's the finest I have ever built, and the next one I build will be even better." She was glad to know this one was it. "And I managed to get not one but two of the most dominant women I've ever seen to stand before me whimpering like the stupid animals that they are."

"You think we're animals now? Wait until you piss us off."

Rayne smiled, thinking that she wouldn't fuck with Bronwyn if she was him. But as she'd pointed out, he was pretty stupid.

"Pissing you off is going to feed me, my dear. Haven't you heard that your blood is like a fine wine to us? That drinking from a tiger is just like a good drug, great sex and fantastic orgasm all at once?" He tisked at her. "And I will drink from you. Drain you when we're finished getting all we can from you."

He walked around them but not close. It didn't matter… when she took him, and she would, she was going to fuck him up regardless of how far away he was. When he stopped near her and sniffed, she saw him back off. Then when he looked at Freddy, she knew that something was wrong.

"Smell something you didn't like? Or are you just realizing that fucking with us is like a fucking fantastic drug, mind-blowing sex and a black you out it was so fan-fucking-tastic great orgasm it's going to be when we kill you?" He sniffed her again.

"It can't be…there's no fucking way. He's dead. I made sure of it. He was supposed to kill him because he'd gone rogue." Rayne looked at Bronwyn, and she shrugged, either not knowing what he was talking about or not caring.

"How do you know Baron Wentcroft? How do you know him, and when was the last time you spoke to him?" She had no idea who he was talking about, but before she could tell him that, he slapped her hard across the face, and blood poured from her lip. "Peter Oliver Wentcroft, my maker, how do you know him?"

Peter? Her Peter? She knew what he meant when he said maker. And it took her several seconds of him standing over her, screaming at her to answer him, for her to realize the man was terrified. She smiled at him and shoved him away from her. He let himself fall, and she walked over to him.

"Peter is my friend, and I last spoke to him this morning just before your idiot flunkies brought me here." She tisked him this time. "He is not going to be happy with you when he figures out what you've been up to, is he?"

"Have you called him yet?" Her mind tried to work around that information. She couldn't call him, could she? He'd told her once that if she needed him, she only needed to think of him. But she'd only used a phone to contact him whenever she needed him. She couldn't reach Neal, but maybe this would work for her.

"Peter, can you hear me?" She let her mind relax and tried again. *"Peter, are you there? It's Rayne, Rayne Golden."*

She stood up, thinking that Jimmy was full of shit, when she felt Peter touch her mind. *"Hello, love. The men are very close to getting past the first wave of guards, and your mate and that of your friend are coming in the way you have let the others out."*

She was so relieved that she nearly forgot why she'd contacted him. *"Do you know a vampire named Jimmy? He said you're his maker."*

"Jimmy? No. It's a very commoner sort of name, isn't it? But I don't recall a child I've made called Jimmy. I knew a…what was his name?"

"He called you Baron Oliver Wentcroft. He said your name was Baron Peter Oliver Wentcroft." She felt his laughter. *"I take it that you remember him."*

"Oh yes. I took him as a lover long ago. Not much of one now that I recall him. Ask him if his name is Theodore James. I called him my Teddy Bear while we…well, let us just leave it at that, shall we?"

"Please, let's do." She heard him laugh again and turned to Jimmy. She smiled at him. He looked grim. "He said your name is Theodore James and that he called you his Teddy Bear. What did you do, Jimmy? Switch around your first and last name so that no

one would know you? You're as stupid as a rock, aren't you?"

He slapped her again. She might not have fallen back so quickly or so hard had she not been bent over so much laughing. When he stood up, she did as well and watched him as he paced.

"He can't enter here. I made sure that no vampires were ever allowed to enter, and I never brought one into the facility. He can't come here to get me." He grinned at her. "And yes, that's just what I did. It made it easier for me to remember my name just after I changed it just before this one. I was forever forgetting what I changed it to before."

"But you don't know that for sure, do you?" He stopped pacing and looked at Bronwyn as she smiled at him. "You don't know for sure that he can't come in here no more than you're sure that a vampire has ever stepped through your doors. But there have been, hasn't there, Freddy? A lot of them, as a matter of fact. You have been working on getting one of them to change you to one of them so you can live on forever."

They all looked at Freddy. "She's lying. You have to know that I'd never do anything to jeopardize this project. It's going to make me…us a great deal of money."

"More than you've stolen from him?" Bronwyn turned to Jimmy again. "He's been making a great deal of money off the bodies that you dump. Did you know that there's a lab not far from here that he is funding with your money?"

Freddy backed up and pressed himself against the wall as Jimmy moved toward him. He kept denying everything even as he was being lifted off the floor with a hand around his throat. When he struggled less and less, Jimmy dropped him to the floor and then jerked him up by his hair and tore his throat out. When he dropped him this time, he moved toward Bronwyn.

"You lied." She shrugged. "I should be impressed, but I'm

not. You just made me kill the only man I had ever trusted before. Well, not trusted so much as used so well." He reached for her, and Rayne touched him. He screamed in pain as he fell back. She moved to stand over him when she felt that Neal was near.

"You're going to pay for that, you fucking bitch." He started to stand up when she put her booted foot on him. He started to rise when he stiffened. Rayne turned to see the man who'd just appeared in the room.

"Ah, there you are." Peter kissed her cheek. "I've been all over this place looking for you two. Was it a necessity that you touch everything as you moved from place to place? I have found where you have taken care of the lab. Bravo for you both. Your mates are on their way up now."

He turned to Jimmy when he started shouting at him. Peter snapped his fingers, and Jimmy's mouth snapped closed almost as loudly. He stood the younger vampire up without so much as lifting his finger.

"You've been behind all of this then. I never would have guessed it of you. Well, that isn't entirely true. I thought you to be a sadist when we were together. It is why I left you on your own. I had hoped that you'd be killed by some farmer or, better yet, fell out into the sunlight to no longer be a concern of mine. Not that you have been, really, but, alas, I should have taken better care to figure out what you were doing and did a great deal more to stop you." He slapped the man. "You've embarrassed me."

"He was the one that hired the man to kill you that night." Jimmy whimpered when Peter looked at her. "He told me that he'd had you killed that day and had thought you dead. When he smelled you on me, he nearly had a kitten."

"A kitten? I don't believe I've heard that one before. A kitten, is it? I'll have to keep that one for my moments when I'm at a loss for...I digress. He wanted me dead." He looked back at Jimmy. "Did you not know that you can feel when I die? You really are a moron, are you not?"

Peter stared at him for a long time, and Rayne wondered what he was thinking. It couldn't bode well for the monster Jimmy, and he was one too. Much worse than even Peter had claimed to be when she'd saved him. When he turned to her, she noticed the hurt in his eyes and felt badly for Peter. This is not what she wanted for her friend to deal with. She wanted to hug him to her, but he stopped her when she stepped forward.

"He has...had a great deal of money that I am giving you." He stopped her before she could tell him she wouldn't take his fucking money. "It is for those that you have saved. See to it that they are taken care of with it."

She nodded. "You're coming back to see me, aren't you, Peter? You're my friend, and I couldn't have survived all those years ago had you not been there for me."

"I'll return, but he must be taken before my maker, and we will...I will be punished for leaving such a child to do what he has done to so many. Even I should have known that something like this was going on and kept tabs on him. He has hurt a great many people and killed many more. I will...he may take back his gift."

"No. No, I won't allow it." He smiled sadly at her. "I mean it, Peter. If he even tries, after all I went through to get that for you, I'll go to him and slice his head off. Or whatever other part of him I can get to. You tell him that I'm going to be gunning for him if he tries."

"You'll do no such thing." He took her hand and kissed it gently. "You are my dearest friend, and no matter what happens, I will forever be in your debt." Then he was gone, and Jimmy with him.

Just as she and Bronwyn were heading for the stairs, they heard someone coming up. It could have been the men, but neither of them was taking any chances. When Neal came through the stairwell first, she dropped the chair she was holding and ran to him.

"You big, stupid cat." He licked her face, and she hugged him even tighter. "What were you planning to put on when you got here? You should think these things through before you execute them."

"The next time you get yourself kidnapped and taken away by a loony man, maybe you could think ahead and tell me that you plan on rescuing yourself, and I won't have to bother being naked when the cops come." He licked her face again. *"And you smell like that fucking vampire again. Didn't we have this discussion once before about you letting men touch you without my permission?"*

"Yes, we did." She sat back on her heels and glanced over at Ryland and Bronwyn holding each other despite one of them being a cat as well. *"You'll just have to mark me again, I suppose. Are you up for it, tiger boy?"*

She purred against his throat when she leaned toward him. He growled low, and she stroked his fur just behind his ears. He'd told her before that it was one of his weakest spots as a cat, and he was nearly rolling over to his back for her when she heard others coming toward them. Standing up, she stood in front of Neal just as five more large cats, one of them a panther, came snarling into the room.

Chapter 14

"So now what?" Rayne looked at him over the drawings she was going over for her meeting with Ryland and the others. "Do you want to get married or not?"

Neal had asked her last night, and she'd not answered him. Of course, he'd been making love to her at the time and had asked her just as she was coming. He should have asked her before they'd gotten home, but he'd been so happy to see her unharmed that he'd completely forgotten. Now the ring seemed to be burning a hole in his pocket.

"Why do you have to marry me? I mean, we already live together thanks to my shop being renovated. All of my clothes are here, and I even added my shampoo to yours on the shelf above our heads. Why you have to have it that high is beyond me." He didn't bother telling her that it was so she'd have to reach up for it, and he liked the way her ass looked when she did it. She'd call him sexist or something again.

He thought opening the car door for her was a perfectly well-mannered thing to do too. It rated right there with him opening the doors for her. She had told him she was capable of doing that as well. And she'd nearly knocked him out when she'd jerked the door from him when he'd done it. He rubbed his forehead where she'd hit him. She was sort of violent when she had a point to make.

"I want you to have my last name." Lame answer, he thought as soon as it came out of his mouth. "And I love you. Isn't that a good enough reason?"

"No. And I love you too. But I see absolutely no reason for us to get married." She snorted. "Most of the people we know already call me Rayne Golden anyway. And if your brother snickers once more when they say it, I'm going to tear his dick off."

He nearly laughed himself. Keith had taken to calling her Rayne Golden Showers for a week now, and no matter how many times he told him that it bothered her, he still insisted on doing it. Maybe Rayne needed to hurt him once just to get him to stop it. But that was beside the point.

"Rayne, I insist that you marry me if for no other reason than you love me." She shook her head, and he stood when she did. "All right, then I won't have sex with you again until you agree."

She leaned in and blew her warm breath against his throat, and he pressed her against the counter. When she nipped his ear lobe, he slipped his hand under her blouse and cupped her breast. She licked the curve of his throat to his mouth and kissed him, his tongue moving along hers like he wanted to move in and out of her. Smooth, long strokes that made him sweat with need.

"You're much too easy, and there isn't any way you'll not have sex with me no matter what you say." He nearly snarled at her, but she had cupped his cock, and he rocked into her hand. "And I have to go to my meeting."

He stood there, gripping the counter so tightly he was sure he was going to leave nail prints in it. When he heard the door open behind him, he turned to see Carl standing there looking a little tight across the mouth like he was trying his best not to laugh.

"Done it again, has she, sir?" Neal nodded. "She is quite the woman, I think. She certainly has you tied up in knots. Told you no again, I suppose?"

"She did. She thinks it's fine the way things are. I don't understand; don't women want you to marry them? I certainly do her." Carl started pulling out breakfast items and arranging them on the counter. "She's been driving me crazy for a week now. And when I finally get to ask her, she turns me down flat. I'm not sure what else to do at this point."

"Perhaps it's not you, sir, but someone else." His heart took a sudden leap when he thought of Peter, and maybe she was in love with him. "Maybe, sir, you should ask her mother what happened that has soured her so much on the idea of marriage."

He sat there for several minutes, trying to remember if she'd ever mentioned her father or her stepfather to him. He couldn't remember if she had or not. She'd mentioned her step-father barking orders but not a word about her real father.

"Her mom was disowned when she found herself pregnant with Rayne. Maybe Karin told her about her life at home. I know nothing about her step-father other than the fact that a couple of the wolves we have working for us liked him." Carl nodded but didn't say anything. "Spill it, old man. What is it you know?"

"I don't really know anything for sure. Men can project any image they want in public, the same as women, I suppose. He may have been a very nice man to the world around him but not nearly so much when he was behind closed doors. Many families have their secrets, sir, even yours." Neal took the plate of food that was offered to him and stared at him for long moments before he spoke.

"Carl, how long have you and your wife worked for me?" He told him nearly ten years. "In all that time, have you ever known me to be anything but an accountant?"

"No, sir, I have not. I have often wondered how you did it all day. Sat at a desk and worked with so many numbers. They are fascinating, I suppose, but for me, I don't think I could do it. I need to create, and I've found that cooking has given me what I need." He handed him a glass of orange juice. "Do numbers give you what you need?"

"They used to." He'd been startled by his own answer and at how quickly he'd answered him. "I've been bored at my job and told Ryland that I needed a break. Maybe what I need is to work my own numbers with a wife."

"You could be right, sir. Nothing like a wonderful wife to make a man rethink what makes him happy." Carl turned and put his arms over his chest and looked at him. "Shall I make arrangements for next weekend for a retirement party for you, sir? I believe it would be just the thing to do."

Neal laughed and told him that would be perfect. "But give me a couple of hours to tell my family I'm quitting first. I think they might be a tad pissy if they found out by being invited to the party."

As he went out to his car, he realized he was whistling. He couldn't remember the last time he'd felt like doing that and decided to turn on the radio as well. He was belting out a tune with it when he felt his phone vibrate in his pocket. Almost reluctantly, he turned the music down and answered his brother Brock's call. But he was laughing so hard he could barely get a thing out of him. He felt himself smiling at the sound and wondered what the hell was going on.

He heard Ryland's name as well as Rayne's. Then he heard some shouting in the background and finally his mother speaking to him. Apparently, she'd taken the phone from Brock.

"You must get down here before he kills her. Though I'm not sure, she might be able to take him and win. Those two fight better than…." He heard her say, "oh dear," then the line went dead.

Pressing a little harder on the gas pedal, he tried to think of all the things that could be going on. For the most part, he wasn't worried. He'd heard too much laughter, and his mom had even sounded like she was having a good time. But the line going dead didn't make him all warm and fuzzy on the inside. He walked in the building and was surprised to see that all the guards were standing near the elevators.

"Something happening?" Stan nodded. "Has this anything to do with the phone call I got from Brock?"

"Maybe. Ryland called down here about three minutes ago and said that we were to stop Miss Rayne from leaving. He said he was coming down after her." Stan looked around and whispered to him as if all the men with him couldn't hear a pin dropping a mile away. "Sorry, sir, but she scares the bedevil out of me and the men. Miss Rayne can…she can make a man wish for his mommy and want to run in the other direction at the same time when she has her back up. And she had it up earlier when she tried to leave here."

So she'd tried to leave. Before he could find out when this had happened, the doors opened, and there she stood. She did have her back up, and she looked ready to do battle with every one of them. One man even took a step back when she lifted her hand to her hair. Then she saw him.

"Did he fucking call you in too? I've never seen a more… did you know that he thinks I'm going to do this job for money and that he thinks he's paying for the renovation on my shop? *My shop*?" She stepped out of the elevator, and every man there let her pass. "I'm going to murder him in his sleep. Do you think he sleeps, or does he just lay there in bed thinking of things just to piss me off?"

"I'll ask Bronwyn the next time I see her. And I work here, in answer to your first question. No one called me." He took her arm and led her to the large conference room where he thought their meeting was going to take place. "Does he know that you're pissed at him and shouldn't have meetings more than a few feet up in the event you need to toss him out the window?"

She laughed but not with humor. "He thinks he's my boss, and…where the hell are we going? I want to go home and think up ways to murder someone."

"I don't think I want to know what he did that would cause you to think such a thing as murder. But I have to ask. How did he manage to piss you off so much in…?" He looked at his watch. "Rayne, you've been here for less than thirty minutes. What the hell happened?"

She sat down and laid her head on the table. "He was bossy. And he said I was being stupid for not wanting him to pay for the renovations."

"You were being stupid, and I do not appreciate you stalking off like a wounded child when I'm speaking to you." Ryland shut the door behind him, but it opened almost immediately when Bronwyn and Brock entered. "I can handle this on my own, thank you. Go back to work."

"Okay, one, you don't talk to me like you do a dog. I do think we've had this discussion before. Two, you will not conduct a meeting where the entire staff is aware that the two of you are screaming at each other like children. Sit down." Everyone sat, including Brock, when Bronwyn pointed to a chair. "This is ridiculous. Adults acting like children. What the hell started this?"

They both started talking at once, and Bronwyn put her fingers in her mouth and let out a whistle that would have broken glass had there been any in the room. She pointed to the chairs again, and both Ryland and Rayne sat. Bronwyn looked at him.

"Do you have anything to say?" He nodded but kept his mouth shut because laughter was close to burbling out, and he was sure she'd hurt him. "Well? What is it?"

He had to take several deep breaths and avoid looking at Brock, who was seated behind Bronwyn and laughing hard. When he looked around the room at the other two, all he could think about was he would miss this.

"I'm turning in my two-weeks notice today." The room erupted in noise, and it took him several seconds to realize they weren't mad at him but congratulating him. "You're not pissed off?"

"Christ, no. I think it's great. So long as I can call on you to help me out once in a while." He nodded at Ryland. There was more he wanted to say, and he figured now was as good a time as any.

"I also want to buy you out on The Pretty Flower. I want to give it to my wife as a wedding gift." Ryland glared at Rayne but nodded. "And there's more. I want you to sign over any and all rights to Dabbler Building. I have a mind that we shouldn't expand but open a second stop, and that will be the perfect place to start."

"Anything else while you're trying to bleed me dry?" Bronwyn slapped Ryland, and he smiled. "You should have bought it yourself long ago when you helped me acquire it for nearly nothing. I'll gift it to you as a wedding gift."

He looked at Rayne. She didn't look any happier now than when she'd come in here with him. He asked his family to leave them for a few minutes, and they'd be up later to finish the project information. She stood up as soon as the door closed. He knew he was in for it by the way she was stalking around the room.

~~~

"I didn't need your help with him. I was going to help him find someone else to do his lobby, and he'd have been just fine. You didn't have to buy that building either. I'm not ready to expand."

"You're not expanding but opening up another shop. And you heard him as well as I did. He gave it to me." She hated it when he was calm when she was pissed.

"I don't have any say in this at all?" He sat on the table while she paced around the room. "You know I can expand, open another shop or anything else I want because it's my shop."

"Of course it is." He smiled at her, and she wanted to bop him in the head. "You should know that as a wedding gift to you, we're going to have to get married, right? I have the ring on me if you'll just say yes."

"I don't want to get married." She felt her face heat up when she realized how loud she'd been. "I just want to live with you."

"Why?" She'd expected him to ask her that, and she had two versions of the same story to tell him. But she found that she couldn't lie to him, not after all that he'd done for her.

"Did you know my step-dad?" He told her he hadn't. "Everyone liked him. Some even said that he was lovable. But he really wasn't. He was mean and hurtful, and he hit my mom."

"What was his reasoning for hurting her?" She looked at him because she'd expected him to ask what she'd done to him. "No man should hit anyone smaller or weaker than them. And no mate should ever hit. Evan should have been taken before his alpha."

"He was the alpha. We tried going over his head, but he'd only shown them the man that people loved and said that my mom was still distraught over the change." Her skin crawled when she thought of the way he'd converted her. "He told her it was his right to change her and that she should have known that before they married."

"He changed her against her will." She nodded. "And when he did it, what did he tell the council when they'd asked him about it? They have rules as we do. Did anyone ask your mom if she wanted to be a wolf?"

His voice had gotten hard, and she took a step back when he came toward her. "You'll not hit me, Neal."

He stopped moving and stared at her. "He hit you, too. He's the.... I wish the motherfucker was still alive because I'd like nothing more than to hunt him down like the animal he was and tear him apart."

"I killed him." He nodded as if he already knew. Hell, for all she knew, he knew how she'd done it. "The snow was coming down hard, and he'd been driving me home from the movies with one of my friends. He wouldn't let me drive, and when I suggested that we walk, he had a fit and said he'd pick us up. After he dropped off my friend, he said it was high time that I became an active member of the pack."

Neal nodded and took a slow step toward her. She knew that if he touched her, she'd never finish the story, and he had to know why she'd never be another man's property.

"He pulled over, and I was jerked from the car, not by him but by several members of the pack. He had them hold me as he took off his belt. He was going to beat me. Then they were all going to take turns biting me until I was changed. He said that if they all did it, then they all could claim me when it was over." Neal took another step toward her. "I...the first man slipped and fell. But I didn't do that, and when one of the others helped him up, I knocked them both down and broke their necks. I don't think the others knew what I'd done until...until later."

"How many, Rayne? How many of them hit you before you

killed them?" She heard his anger and was afraid. She told him three more men besides the two she'd killed.

"I murdered them all and then put them into the car. It was easy enough for me to drive it back down the road and park the car near the top of the bend and wait. The snow was coming down hard enough by then that the tracks were all gone, and the place where they'd hurt me was covered up. Once there were no tracks, I put the car into gear and made it go over the railing and into the ravine at the bottom. I walked back to my friend's house and spoke to her and then left."

He asked her what she'd told her. "Nothing. I just…she thought we'd walked there, and I walked the rest of the way home, and Mom was on the couch. It wasn't until a couple of days later that they found them."

He touched her then. He ran his hand down her arms to her hand and laced his fingers into hers. He held her that way for several minutes until he lifted her chin up and kissed her. She felt his love for her all the way to her toes.

"I'm not like him." She tried to pull away, but he wouldn't let her. "I'm not like any of them. I'm in love with you, and you love me, but that's beside the point." He took the ring out of his pocket and slipped it on her right hand and not her left. "I want to marry you, but I can understand why you won't."

"But you'll keep at me about it, won't you?" He shook his head. "I don't understand. You don't want me anymore?"

"Oh, I want you. I want to spend the rest of my life with you, and if you won't marry me but stay with me, then I'll have to learn to live with that. But I won't ask you again either. I need for you to tell me when you're ready, and I'll be there." He kissed her gently on the mouth. "I love you with all my heart and will always and forever keep you in my heart, but I won't force you to do anything that you're not comfortable with. I want you to trust me."

She nodded. She did trust him. She just didn't ever want to marry him. Taking a step back, she walked to the trolley that had some water bottles on it and picked one up. She wasn't thirsty but needed something to do with her hands.

"What about the shop? Are you going to still buy your brother out?" He told her he was. "But it will be yours then and not mine."

"No. Even if you don't marry me, I still want you to have it." He wrapped his arms around her waist and held her to him. "I give it to you. Would you like to see what I have as a plan to expand in another five years?"

She nodded, and they sat at the table. He had written out a five-year plan with projections of spending and also a way for them to make more money. He'd never once called it his business, and he never ordered her to do what he'd said. She would, however, because it was a good plan and a safe one. She liked safe.

"And if you wouldn't mind, I'd still like to work with you in the shops as well as do the books. I'm unemployed now and will need to keep busy or drive you nuts. Besides, your mom said you were doing them anyway, and I'd like to keep you busy in the showroom while I help you manage the money."

She thought of what Ally had said about her and Alistair working together and wondered if that would happen to them. Christ, she hoped so. She'd just have to make sure she had someone who could run the register while they were having their own bit of fun.

Chapter 15

Peter stood near the building for nearly an hour before he could work up the nerve to go and see her. He could see her inside the building running around while people came and went, nearly all of them with trays of plants. When Rayne came out and walked toward him, he nearly disappeared but held his ground.

"You going to stand out here all evening, or were you going to jump us as we left for the day?" He started to protest when she laughed. "I'm kidding. Why don't you come inside? We'll be closing soon anyway."

"You called him." She stood still while he continued. "He told me that you called him and told him if he took your gift, you'd hunt him down. Are you aware of what he could do to you if he had wanted to?"

"Yes. But as I said to you before you left me that you were my friend and that if he even considered it, I would hurt him." He nodded. "Did he take it from you?"

"I gave it to him for a period of one year." She growled low, and he laughed. "But he would not accept it. He said that while he was not afraid of you, he did respect you for what you'd been to me."

"He's a good man too." Peter nodded at her. "So you're still a day walker, but you still won't come to see Neal. That's not very nice of you."

"I have to go back to him. Tonight. I have to...I have a fine to pay, and I must pay it. But I have...he gave me this night to ask a favor of you."

"How long?" He knew she'd want to know and was nearly not going to tell her, but she'd find out soon enough. "How long will you have to stay away from your beloved plants?"

He looked at her sharply. "You are too smart for your own good, and it may get you into some trouble someday. You should heed my advice and—"

"How long, Peter?" He looked into her shop and saw there were two beings, people that were not quite human there that he'd never seen before.

"I cannot have them for a decade." He looked at her. "I would ask that you'd care for them for me. The seeds of life that you gave me have sprouted true leaves, and I have ten growing now. And the others...the other seeds you have given me, they fill my rooms of my home fully."

"You know that I'll care for them for you." He nodded. "Will you have your cell phone with you where you're going?"

"Yes. It is not as if I'm being punished in staying with him. I will be like a king, just without a castle of my own."

And a king without a true friend. And she had been to him for more years than any other being had been. He tried his best to think of something happy to tell her, but all he could think about was not seeing her for a whole ten years.

"When you return, what will you do?" He shrugged, too depressed to think what he'd do. "You'll have a job working for me if you want it."

"You'd have me work for you? With your plants and other...
humans?" She laughed and told him yes. "Do you believe that to
be wise? I am still a vampire."

"And you will forever be my friend." She pulled out her cell
phone when it rang, and she looked at him with a smile. "I have
just heard, my lord. And while I understand what you've done, I
don't like it."

He was afraid of who she might be talking to. Peter knew
it was his maker, and he was asking when he was returning. He
should have been there over two hours ago. He looked at the little
girl running in the parking lot with her purchase. She was so happy
that he had to smile. He felt the same way when he was given
something that grew by his care. He looked back at Rayne when
she handed him her phone. Viktor started speaking as soon as he
put the device to his ear.

"There are a great many people in this world that I like. Less
that I love. And fewer more that I respect. Your friend is one of the
few. She loves you dearly, I think." Peter nodded, then realized
that Viktor could not see him.

"She is a true and wonderful friend. And though she does not
tell you often, I believe she enjoys you as well." He looked at
Rayne as she moved toward the little girl who had just dropped
her flower and spilled it out. "I shall be there momentarily, sir. I
have been...it's more difficult than I would have thought to tell her
goodbye."

"I'm sure that it would be." He chuckled slightly, and Peter
wanted to tell him not to laugh at him at a time like this. "You
should also know that she is going to be harder on you than I
would have been."

"Sir?" He watched her still as she took the little girl inside and
sat her on the counter as her mother stood by. After a Band-Aid

was put onto the wound at her knee, the little girl was given a new plant that was slightly bigger than the other and a hug.

"She's going to be your guardian whilst you serve your sentence for me." His heart took a strange beat as his maker continued. "I will visit you from time to time to be assured that you are not visiting *your* flowers and such, but she assures me that I have nothing to worry about."

He didn't understand the emphasis on the word "your," but he was still trying to work out what he was being told. And not to get his hopes up too much if what he was thinking wasn't true.

"Are you saying that I've no need to come there for the decade?" He held his breath as he waited for him to answer. Rayne was walking toward him again, and he realized that he was in love with the young faerie.

"Yes, that's what I'm saying. She drives a hard bargain, but in the end, I believe I will be getting the better end of the deal. I won't have to see you moping around as you think of your plants."

"She…what will she owe you, sir? I would ask that you not tax her overly much. She does not have much, but she is a good woman. The entire Golden family is." He laughed again, and Peter smiled. "You know this already."

"I do, but I'm glad to hear that you know it as well. Her tax will be nothing. She did not beg me, but…I should like to meet her one day. Not by email or calls as we have done so much of recently, but actually meet her." Peter nodded again and reached for Rayne's hand. "You will have a list of jobs to perform for her as well as me. Some of them will be easy for a man like you. The rest…well, we shall see, shan't we?"

After a few more minutes of them setting up their first meeting, he handed Rayne back her phone. "You have saved me from being bored. I don't know what to say."

"You say 'thank you, Rayne' and let it go. And you'll be here tomorrow morning bright and early to begin your work for me." She handed him a tee shirt that he hadn't noticed before. "You'll wear one of these every day when you come in. You might not like the colors, but I want you to stand out if people need you."

The shirt was an overly bright pink, and when she waved it at him, it nearly made him ill. But he took it like it was a badge of honor. She nodded and told him that she'd see him in the morning and to go home.

"But I cannot see my plants." She walked back to him and put out her hand. He looked at it, then at her.

"Sell them to me." He started to shake his head, not understanding her. "Sell them to me for whatever I have in my pocket, and they'll no longer be your plants but mine. And you'll have to care for them as I don't have the time to be messing with them."

He took her hand, then jerked her body to his to hug her. He had never been so happy in his life. He had his friends, a job, and now he was going to be able to see his…no, *her* plants daily. They struck their bargain, and she returned to the shop and he to his home. He sat in the room with the new seedlings until the sun rose. He was going to work. He'd already written out her receipt for a dollar and twelve cents for his flowers, all the money she had on her.

~~~

"He touched you." She looked up at Neal as he leaned against the doorjamb where she was working. "You let that vampire touch you to his body, and now you smell like him."

Her body responded to his voice, not so much his words. When he stood up and moved toward her, she could see his cat race along his skin. When he stood over her, she felt her cat purr just below the surface, and she rubbed her head over his belly.

"Is there a way for me to make it up to you?" She didn't move when he pulled her rubber band out of her hair. "Is everyone gone?"

"It doesn't matter if they are or not. You've been bad." Her cat snarled at him, and she let her go just a little, and he yanked her hair back. "Behave, or this will go worse for you."

Worse could only be better with him. She groaned when he lifted her up. "Neal, I'm so sorry. I won't misbehave again.'

"Yes, you will. And we both know it." She didn't nod because he was in the mood to play, and so was she. "Did you bring any extra clothes and put them in the apartment like I asked you to?"

"Yes," she managed to hiss out when he bit her in the shoulder. "I put them with yours and some wine in the refrigerator. Christ, Neal, I'm soaking wet."

He tore her clothes from her. Not gently either, but using his claws, he shredded them into long strips until she was naked. Lifting her by her ass, he sat her on her workbench and took her breast into his mouth.

He suckled so hard that she thought for sure he was going to take all of her into his mouth. When he pinched her other nipple, she wrapped her legs around his hips and pulled him to her. His cock was so hard that she could feel herself getting wetter.

He stepped back a little without letting go of her breast and opened his shirt. Buttons bouncing off the pots made a tinkling sound. When he unsnapped his pants and freed his cock, she reached down and wrapped her hand around him.

"Do you have any idea how wild it makes me when you smell like another male?" She told him it was why she let him hug her. "Fuck, you're evil. I'm going to enjoy this."

He entered her hard, his cock slamming into her so deeply that she cried out. When he took her mouth, she sucked his tongue into her and toyed with it like she wanted to do to his cock.

He lifted his head. "My cat wants to fuck yours. But I can't seem to stop." He pressed her back on the table and held himself still in her as he ran his hands up and down her ribs and over her breast. His cock rode her slowly, and she wanted to scream at him to finish her. Her clit was so needy of his touch that she reached down to slide her hands over her.

"No." He held her hand away. "Not yet. I want to make you pay for teasing me. Making me wild for you. When I come, I'm going to pull out and come all over you and then use it to bring you to peak."

He continued to tease her body, leaning over and nipping at her flesh and then licking the tiny wound better. When he pulled her tighter against him, she felt his cock stretch, but when he suddenly pulled from her, she sat up.

His cock exploded on her. As he fisted himself in long, quick strokes, streams of hot cum splashed on her breasts and hung from her nipples and belly until she was covered in him. When he pressed her back again, he buried his mouth over her pussy and bit her just enough that she cried out. Begging him for her own release, he suckled her clit into this mouth and fucked her with his fingers. Her climax roared from her, and her cat snarled.

Her body was still reacting to her release as tremors shook her. He lifted his head, and she could see the cat roll over him and stayed very still, knowing what he was going to do. As soon as his giant cat stood where the man had, he, too, bit into her flesh, giving her so much that she cried out from it. When he moved away from her, she could see his erection, and her cat snarled again as she let her take her.

The shift was painless, but he was on her in seconds. As he took her to the floor, she tried her best to crawl from beneath him as he bit down into her shoulder. Even as he entered her, she knew that he was not just marking her but claiming her. Her cat tried once more to move, but he bit her until she stilled.

"Christ, do you have any idea what it does for him when you let him taste you like that?" Neal moaned. *"He loves your taste and you. My cat is in love with you as a human."*

His cock pistoned in her, and she tried to meet each of his thrusts, but he was too quick, his body too heavy. When he released her from his mouth, he roared as he held her with his enormous paws and filled her.

He shifted back first, and as she lay there watching him walk around, she stood up and walked to him and rubbed her head on his thigh. She licked him there and then sank her teeth into him. He cried out and held still as she tore at his flesh and held there. When she was finished, she shifted before she knelt down and licked the wound closed and looked up at him.

"She wanted to mark you." He nodded. "Is that right? I didn't know what she was going to do until she was already doing it."

"Yes. She...the female, as far as I know, rarely marks her mate." They both looked down at the scar already forming. "I'll wear this proudly."

She nodded, and they walked through the office to the apartment in the back and dressed. He lay on the bed while she told him what had happened with Peter.

"So he'll get to take care of the plants he loves so much and work with you as well. Sounds like a win-win for him." She shook her head. "What doesn't he know yet?"

"He has to disperse the money that Jimmy left behind." He cocked his brow at her. "Did I tell you how much there was? Just over five billion dollars. He has to help others with it and keep track of what he spends it on and how much."

"He'll need my help then?" She shrugged. "Did you think I wouldn't want to help him? He's my friend too."

"I know that, and he loves you dearly, but…well, he might not ask you at first, and I don't want you to offer either." She pulled on a tee-shirt, thinking that they'd just nap here before going home. "His maker will come to visit us from time to time to make sure that he's doing a good job."

She had told him that there was no doubt in her mind that Peter would do an amazing job, but he'd laughed at her. She told Neal.

"He wasn't laughing at you, love. He was laughing because you felt you needed to tell him that. I think he knows Peter just as well as you do." She nodded at him. "But does he know that you sold him the plants? Will he be upset with you for how you maneuvered around him?"

"It was his idea." They both laughed, and she went to the little kitchen and brought him back the wine and other treats she'd put there. "Did you know what else he told me? I get paid for watching over him. He didn't say how much, but he said it would come to me monthly by courier. I thought I'd just give it back to Peter so he could have a paycheck. He said he doesn't need money as he has been around for a while."

Neal took the cracker and cheese she offered him and took a sip of the wine. "How old is he anyway? Has he ever told you?"

"He is nearly sixty thousand years old. He and his maker came here from their own place when this country was still a babe. Peter told me that once they'd gotten here, they explored for a long time before he settled here and his maker in Europe." She took a sip from his glass as she continued. "Peter said that place they come from is beautiful and is run by Viktor's father."

"And where is his home at?" She looked away and then smiled at him. "I don't think I like that look. You're going to tell me that they're from another planet, aren't you?"

"No, not a planet, but another realm. He and his maker came from a realm that is as far from here as our moon is and…I can't remember the rest, but I believe him."

Neal nodded and laid back. "I gave Peter my blood when we were going to rescue you. He said that I have a great deal of you in me."

She laid over him and yawned. "And what does that mean? That you're going to be a faerie like me?"

He didn't answer her right away, and she thought he'd fallen asleep. When he finally did speak, she looked up at him and felt a shiver of fear. What he was telling her couldn't be true.

"He said that I'm more you than you're me. He said that when we have a child, it will be more of both of us than we are." He pulled her closer to his chin. "He said that forevermore we would breed the new race of beings."

He was telling them they were immortal or that they'd have a shit ton of kids before they were too old to have any more. But she didn't ask him, and he didn't continue. She lay there for a long time after he started to snore softly. Getting up, she went to her flowers and worked with them instead of thinking about what might have been said.

By the time Neal woke and the first truck was pulling in, she'd planted the entire order for the lobby of the Golden Towers as well as the plants for the law firm of Gable and Son. Peter showed up a little before six, and all three of them unloaded the truck in less than two hours.

"There's a driver on the phone. Says he has a backload for you if you want it." Rayne looked at Neal when he came around the corner when her mom told her about the trucker. "He said that he can sell it to you for less than before because it's a full load."

"How much less?" Her mom handed Neal the phone, and he talked for only a few minutes before hanging up. "We have some merchandise coming."

She didn't care for his grin. "How much merchandise, and where am I supposed to put it? You do know that we only have this showroom and the parking lot, right?"

"He's going to take it to the Dabbler Building for now. We'll need to invest in a bigger truck to haul it back and forth." She nodded and waited for him to tell her how much. "We should really think about expanding now."

"How much merchandise?" He laughed. "Neal, I can and will hurt you. How much are we getting and why?"

"You remember the place that was in competition with you for our lobby?" She nodded. "They just closed down without notice. Apparently, you were never in competition with them so much as the other way around. You put them under. We're getting their inventory and anything else we want from their defunct store for only ten cents on the dollar. He needs to unload it."

"I don't understand. The whole store is ours?" He nodded. "And it's for sale, all the merchandise?"

"Yes. What are you thinking?" This time she smiled at him, and he frowned. "I don't think I want to know."

"Call him back and tell him we'll buy it all for twenty cents on the dollar and to leave it there. Can I borrow enough money to buy the shop?" She knew the moment he figured out what she meant.

"Hell yes." He picked up the phone, and after fifteen minutes, she had a deal. She nearly fell over when he told her how much. "You can do this, Rayne. I swear to you. It's just a little faster than we had planned, but it's perfect. The location it...what is it?"

"How am I going to pay you back? That's...Christ, did you say seven hundred thousand? As in seven and five zeros? I only paid fifty for this place."

She hyperventilated while he laughed. When they loaded into their car and drove to the other shop, she was amazed at all the merchandise that came with it. Walking around, she could already see where she'd put everything, and when Neal told her the trucks were coming in now, she turned to look at him. He had made this possible without asking for anything in return. She loved this man.

"Will you marry me?"

About the Author

Kathi Barton, the author of the bestselling series Force of Nature, lives in Nashport, Ohio, with her husband, Paul. In addition to writing full-time, Kathi likes to spend time with her eight grandkids, three children and three children-in-laws. She writes to relax and have fun.

Her muse, a cross between Jimmy Stewart and Hugh Jackman, brings them to life for her readers in a way that has them coming back time and again for more. Her favorite genre is paranormal romance with a great deal of spice. You can visit Kathi online and drop her an email if you'd like. She loves hearing from her fans. aaronskiss@gmail.com.

Follow Kathi on her blog: http://kathisbartonauthor.blogspot.com/

www.ingramcontent.com/pod-product-compliance
Lightning Source LLC
Chambersburg PA
CBHW022109170626
46808CB00002B/659